Sing for a Gentle Rain

Sing for a
Gentle Rain
J. Alison James

ATHENEUM   **NEW YORK**

Collier Macmillan Canada
Toronto

Maxwell Macmillan International Publishing Group
New York   Oxford   Singapore   Sydney

Atheneum
Macmillan Publishing Company
866 Third Avenue
New York, NY 10022

Collier Macmillan Canada, Inc.
1200 Eglinton Avenue East
Suite 200
Don Mills, Ontario M3C 3N1

Printed in the United States of America
   2   3   4   5   6   7   8   9   10
Designed by Nancy B. Williams

Library of Congress Cataloging-in-Publication Data
James, J. Alison.
   Sing for a gentle rain/by J. Alison James.—1st. ed.
      p.   cm.
   Summary: A boy's search for an explanation to a persistent dream
leads him to an Anasazi cliff village, 700 years ago, where a lovely
young Indian girl needs his help to ensure the survival of her people.
   ISBN 0-689-31561-9
   1. Pueblo Indians—Juvenile fiction.   [1. Pueblo Indians—Fiction.
2. Indians of North America—Fiction.   3. Space and time—Fiction.]
I. Title.
PZ7.J15412Si   1990   90-639
[Fic]—dc20   CIP
                                                                    AC

In memory of my mother

If there were water
And no rock
If there were rock
And also water
And water
A spring
A pool among the rock
If there were the sound of water only
Not the cicada
And dry grass singing
But sound of water over a rock
Where the hermit-thrush sings in the
  pine trees
Drip drop drip drop drop drop drop
But there is no water

T. S. Eliot, *The Waste Land*
(lines 346–359)

Acknowledgments

I am tremendously grateful to Winston Hurst, director of the Edge of the Cedars Museum, for checking the historical accuracy of this manuscript. I would also like to thank Tom Vaughn and Michael Williams at the Anasazi Heritage Center for their help in my research.

For their support in the writing of this book, I would like to thank Nancy Bond, Mary Lee Donovan, Margaret McElderry, and Marcia Marshall.

Last of all, I would like to thank my family: Barbara Lucas, Nathanael and Anika James, for their loving patience.

Sing for a Gentle Rain

THE BEGINNING

Spring Rain stood at the rim of the mesa, looking out across her world. The sky stretched empty, cloudless, across expanses to reach the unrisen sun. She stood straight, unclothed, her unwrapped hair covering her back like a blanket. She waited for the first edge of sun to push up out of the dry earth. It would come, soon, but not quite yet.

From this high up, she could see the patterns of drought. She saw the river bed, now just a snake marking in the sand. Anasan, her grandfather, told tales of when the valley was green with trees, but now only rugged juniper broke the monotony of the dust-red wasteland. Even the animals had gone, following the smell of rain.

Her village needed to go. They had one final journey before they completed their cycle, and they could not survive here much longer. But they could not go until they had the leader, the one who could see the path. By birthright, Spring Rain should have been the one. But she was a girl. Now, for lack of anything else to do, she

1

sang chants of power to the rising sun and prayed for rain.

The sun pushed through the earth, just an edge. Spring Rain lifted her clear voice through the sky to greet it. She sang words more ancient than the tribe itself, words from the very beginning of life, when people lived beneath the crust of the earth.

She had no real idea of what she sang. She had never been taught to understand these words. But as she sang, she hoped for rain, a sweet, gentle rain that would fill the land with the green of life. Such a rain she had never seen, but her grandfather told her how the desert blossoms after a spring rain.

And she sang for a son, for the one to lead the tribe out of the wilderness, to the land where the green river rushes by the fertile fields.

CHAPTER I

James was awake, but he kept his eyes closed tight, trying to recall his dream. It flitted around the edges of his thoughts and broke apart, leaving him frustrated and thirsty. He got up to get a glass of water.

In the kitchen, Grandad was already perking coffee and frying bacon. He looked at James's worn jeans and crumpled T-shirt with disapproval. "I know," said James, "but in my day, everybody wears T-shirts, especially in this weather." The temperature was already seventy-eight degrees, and the sun was still low in the sky. James stuck bread in the toaster and got out the plates. "Sleep well?" he asked.

"Well enough." Grandad sat down at the table. "I woke up about three, read a bit, and went back to sleep." He scooped out his egg from the shell, carefully nestling it on his toast. "It's a new book about the Mayan religious rites. It did the trick."

"You mean it put you back to sleep?"

Grandad nodded. "You're late this morning," he commented.

"I know," James said. "I had a dream that went away before I could remember it. I stayed in bed trying to bring it back."

"Never works," said Grandad.

James picked up his pack and was out the door with his toast still in his hand. "See you later," he shouted through the screen.

His grandfather waved, shooing him off like a fly.

James looked back at the house he had lived in all his life. Ever since he was three, when his mom started touring with her band, he and Grandad had lived there alone. The house was just right for the two of them.

James had to leave early since his high school was thirty miles away. He drove his truck by the elementary school to pick up his friend, but Rocco had already left on the high school bus. James turned on to U.S. 191 and headed north. It was good to have a half hour to himself before the onslaught of classes.

James wasn't very popular, mostly through his own choice. He was good looking, with the straight black hair and high cheekbones of his Indian father, and with his mother's bright green eyes. But he wasn't interested in the girls who came after him. They seemed fake and self-conscious. He hung out with some of the Navajos, like Rocco, but even though they accepted him, he didn't really fit in. When he needed to talk, he talked to Grandad, and when there was something he couldn't say to him, it was too private for anyone.

James was almost finished with his junior year, and if he managed to pass the classes he hated, he'd be done with school next year. He wasn't poring over college catalogs the way some juniors were. He figured he'd work a couple of years before he decided where he wanted to go and what he wanted to study. He had to go to college eventually. His grandfather was big on education.

As James pulled into the parking lot at San Juan High, he tried to surprise his mind into remembering his dream. But all he could get was a haunting sense of dry heat and thirst. He'd never had such a powerful reaction to a dream before. Usually if he didn't wake up remembering, it was gone, and that was that.

He was thinking about it again during fifth period when Mrs. Twitchell's brassy voice broke through his concentration. "James?" He looked up.

"I was asking if you had decided on the subject of your final project. You and Rocco are the last ones to submit a proposal."

Good old Rocco, James thought. *He never makes up his mind either.*

"Well, James?"

"Uh, no," he answered. He had managed to avoid thinking about this project until it was as good as forgotten, and he had absolutely no ideas.

"If I may remind you of the assignment, you are to do a sociological study of any culture you choose, provided it is not your own. I realize it may not have occurred to you that there are others."

Some people in the class snickered.

James hesitated. "Uh, yeah," he said. "Sure. How about the ancient Mayans and their religious rites." He quoted the title of his grandfather's book. It was a little rash, because Grandad was obviously in the middle of reading it, and he sometimes took over a month with one book, checking for accuracy. But it took care of the problem for the moment. Mrs. Twitchell looked a bit surprised, shook her head, and continued.

"Rocco? Rocco Tossi?"

James went back to his dream.

At home that afternoon, James went into the living room to find his grandfather. It looked more like a library—the walls were bookshelves, and books were lying open on the sofa and tables. It was Grandad's collection, piled up from years of anthropological research.

He was in the easy chair with his eyes closed. The Mayan book was lying open in his lap, and his fingers were moving back and forth on the page. He was thinking. James sat down at the piano. He touched the keys lightly, playing a tune that was in his mind. He had had lessons when he was little, but now he just liked to run through sounds.

After playing for a while, James knew Grandad was listening. "Grandad," he said, "I have to do a report on another culture. It's my last assignment of the year, and the teacher was getting on my case today because I haven't even picked out a topic yet." He didn't mention the Mayan idea, because Grandad was obviously using the book.

Grandad was quiet for a moment, then asked, "When is this report due?"

James smiled, his fingers trailing on the keys, playing notes without music. "Next week."

Grandad grunted getting out of his chair. "Play something nice," he said. So James turned back to the piano, and Grandad went to the shelves and selected several books. He put them on the piano and went into the kitchen. "Want some iced tea?" he called.

"Thanks." James looked through the pile. There was a thick book on the Aztec culture and myths, a paperback on the language origins of the Caribbean islands, a traveler's account of a tribe in the Philippines previously unvisited by white people, and a slim volume on the ritual and customs of the Anasazi. James had heard of them. A map inside the cover showed that the Anasazi were a prehistoric people from the Four Corners area, where Utah, Arizona, New Mexico, and Colorado all meet. James sat down on the sofa and started leafing through, looking at the pictures of the people to see how they lived.

The only photographs in the book were of artifacts and ruins, but there were drawings throughout of people working and playing. James paused at one picture of kids in a village. He tried to imagine what it would be like to be one of those kids. All of a sudden he felt a wave of heat and dizziness. He closed his eyes.

"Are you all right?" Grandad set the tea down on the table next to James.

"Yeah." He took the tea and drank it thirstily. "Yeah. I just got dizzy for a minute."

Grandad put his hand on James's forehead. "It's awfully hot out today," he said. He noticed what James was reading. "What do you think of the book?" he asked.

"It seems pretty good." James smiled at Grandad. "And it's got good pictures.

"It is good up to a point," said Grandad, "but you have to watch out. From what I know of that fellow, he strings together assorted facts for the sake of an overall picture. He's a better storyteller than he is an archaeologist."

"But most of this is true, isn't it? He couldn't make up all this stuff, could he?"

"It's impossible to be certain of anything when a culture has left no written record of itself. Just take what he says with a cup of salt."

James was reading it again when he went to bed that night. He fell asleep with the book on his pillow. In the early morning, the same dream called loudly into his subconscious. When he woke up, with a parched throat and the remnants of a whispered song, the pages of the book were glued to his forehead by sweat. Half asleep, he looked at the picture where the book had fallen open. A ring of ancient Indians were dancing in front of their cliff village. His eyelids drooped and music for their dancing swarmed up from his sleep. But the electronic buzz of his alarm clock shattered the music. Now the characters in the book were just ink on paper. Disappointed, he headed off for the bathroom to splash water on his face.

CHAPTER II

The sun was up, and the village would be stirring. The air was still sharply chilled, for the heat of summer hadn't stretched into the early morning yet. In another moon, it would be warm from sunup to sundown. Spring Rain scrambled down the cliff and took her place by the women to grind corn for the morning. She hated this work, but now that she was a woman, it was expected of her. The women gossiped; Atoko and Raina argued about whether Raina should lie with her man when he stayed in the kiva until the night was half spent.

Spring Rain felt awkward, outside the conversation. She had been with the women through the winter, but up until this past harvest, she had denied being a girl. Anasan wanted a boy for the singing, so she pushed herself to be the best at everything boys were supposed to do. It wasn't hard—the competition was Kyaro, and he was three summers younger. So she was the best archer, best trap setter, best weaver. The village ignored her attempts; they knew sooner or later she'd have to come around.

And she did—at the last Corn Harvest moon. She remembered the shock of discovery. She had felt pain in her belly through the night, and in the morning she lay in bed, reluctant to get up. She lived with her grandfather, Anasan, who was also the Healer.

Anasan put his cool hand on her stomach, feeling for what was wrong. Then he saw a streak of blood on her legs, and his concern vanished.

"So that's your trouble." His words were laughing. "I have no medicine for this problem, only a blessing." He stood her up and put his arms on her shoulders. They were the same height now. "For this you don't see me. Go and talk to Sorsi Raina. Tell her that today you become a woman."

Spring Rain opened her mouth to protest, but closed it again. Anasan went on, "After seven nights, when you come back from the women's hut, we will have a finishing ceremony for you."

Spring Rain turned away from Anasan, and her tears blurred the path to the ladder. She was not ready to be a woman. She enjoyed the freedom of being the oldest child. She took care of the children. She worked with fibers to make baskets and clay to make pots, but she was still allowed to make mistakes. The women had to polish each piece to perfection.

"Take joy!" he shouted after her as she went along the narrow ridge in the cliff. "Now you are ready to bear a son; the meaning of the songs will be revealed to him, and the village will leave the dry land."

Anasan's hut was high in the overhanging cliff cave, perched precariously at the wide end of a long ledge. To get down to the village, Spring Rain had to climb down what were really only chips in the rock until she reached the ladder. The village houses were stacked like steps, one on top of another, with ladders leading from one roof to the next. One house had three levels, and it was from this highest roof that the ladder leaned against the wall. Spring Rain had been climbing up and down since she was able to walk, and thought nothing of scaling the cliff. Anasan was too old and stiff to climb much anymore. He had to stay in his hut and depend on Spring Rain to bring him food and news from the village.

She found Sorsi Raina sitting with a group, grinding corn on the flatstones. Spring Rain tried to tug on her arm. She wanted to talk alone, but the other women noticed how upset she was and pestered her with questions.

"What's wrong, Spring Rain?"

"If there were any boys in the village, I'd think it was boy trouble."

"Nonsense. Spring Rain is too young for boys. She's still a boy herself."

She was not—that was the whole trouble. Tears stung her eyes. The women looked at each other with new understanding.

Raina stood up, brushing off her hands. "So today is your day?" Spring Rain nodded. "Congratulations. It's taken you long enough. This next winter will be your fifteenth. I was only eleven when I became a woman. I had Kyaro when I was your age."

They all started talking about when they first became

women, and their words took a rhythm from the grinding stones. Raina stood up to go with Spring Rain.

"Wait," said old Atoko. "She looks like she feels the pain." Spring Rain nodded, stopping new tears with an effort. Atoko went into the hut behind her and came back with a small clay pot. "The peddler brought these seeds from far away. Anasan made them into a drink for women with the moon pains and for childbirth. Finish this drink, but take only one mouthful at a time. Then a little later, take another."

Spring Rain nodded her thanks and followed after Raina. The women's hut was on the far side of the village, separated from the other homes by a low ledge of stones. Once a month every woman from the village spent a few days in here. Raina told her that this was when they were unclean. They could not bleed in the village or it would bring infertility to themselves, to their animals, and to their harvest.

The hut was empty. There were two beds of dried brush covered over with a woven blanket. The fire pit was dark and cold. Raina made up a small fire, then left her, saying, "Just lie down quietly, Spring Rain, and you'll feel better. I'll come by later when my work is done."

Then she was alone. She took a taste of the bitter tincture, then she just lay still, pressing her fist against her teeth to calm the pain. Her whole body ached. Finally after another swallow, the pain abated, and she was able to sleep.

She felt better when she woke up. She lay on her back and looked around at the walls of the hut. She had only been inside this hut two times before: once when she was born—her mother had died here—and once when Raina gave birth to Kyaro. The hut had seemed large and mysterious then, full of secrets. She was only three winters old, and Raina was the one who cared for her. Since Spring Rain's own mother had died giving her birth, Raina was her mama. When it was time for Raina to have her baby, Spring Rain followed along to help her. The other women told her to run and play, but she waited until they were busy, slipped by, and hid in a dark corner.

She could remember it all so clearly, as if she were three again and seeing it for the first time. There were women around Raina, holding her up. Her belly was moving. Spring Rain didn't know then that Kyaro was living in there. Raina was gasping, like a runner in the hot wind. Then she moaned. She was in a square of light from the doorway, and when she squatted down, Spring Rain could see a hole open between her legs. There was a rush of liquid, and Raina screamed again. Spring Rain wanted to run and comfort her, but she could only press her hands against her ears and watch as if paralyzed. A tiny foot dangled from the hole. Atoko sang out encouragement, held on to the foot, and pulled.

Spring Rain looked on in horror. She realized all at once that this was a baby. This was being born, and this was how her mother had died. The thought was too much for her. She squeezed her eyes, pushed her hands against her ears, and let out a whimper. Just at that moment there was silence in the room while the mother took a breath. Their faces all turned to where

Spring Rain hid in the corner. "Take her away," cried Raina, then she screamed like a coyote and out shot the other foot.

Spring Rain didn't wait to be taken away. She fled from the room and ran and ran, her hands still pressed against her ears. She cried as loudly as she could to cover the sounds of Raina's pain.

Someone picked her up before she ran off the edge of the cliff. Someone strong gathered her in his arms and pressed her to his bare chest. Slowly she let her head rest against her grandfather's familiar shoulder, and he sang to her. Still holding her, he climbed up the ladders to his hut above the village.

When she was settled on her little bed next to his long one, he touched her eyes and said slowly, "You see too much, child."

Spring Rain closed her eyes again, remembering the safety of her grandfather's arms.

She had understood then why his words, which felt so harsh that morning, were truly a blessing. Finally now, perhaps the line of old ones could be continued. That line, which was stopped so suddenly at her mother's death, could be finished with a son by Spring Rain. Only she needed a man to lie with. Sons don't come on their own.

CHAPTER III

Hey, James, you skuzzball!" Rocco came up from behind and dropped a handful of dead grass down the back of James's shirt.

"Cut it out." James swung his arm out around behind himself and missed. Rocco sat down on the grass. It was their lunch period.

"How come you were so quiet in Twitchell's class today?" Rocco asked. Mrs. Twitchell had, as usual, let fly several sarcastic remarks at both of them, but only Rocco had taken the bait.

"I don't know," said James. "I was bored."

"You were more than bored," said Rocco. "You were dead in your seat. Hey, amigo, I need your support in that class. You can't just dry up on me. You've been this way for a whole week too. What's up with you? Sick or something?"

What could he say? That he's had this recurring dream that he can't even remember, but it bugs the hell out of him? That he's been reading this book about the

Anasazi that sings songs in his brain? What would Rocco say to that?

"This social studies project is bullshit," he finally said.

"Totally," said Rocco. "Have you done anything?"

"No way," said James truthfully. He hadn't looked at that Mayan book, and he didn't want to think about doing a phony report on the Anasazi one. "When's it have to be done by?"

"Tuesday," said Rocco.

"Great. That gives us the weekend at least."

"Not me," said Rocco. "I have to help my brother-in-law down at the trading post. He's all alone there."

"What's wrong with your sister?"

"What's wrong? She's eight months pregnant, and the doctor said she had to take it easy."

"Right, I forgot," said James. "So what's it going to be, a Monday night job?"

"A two-page *D,*" said Rocco. He stood up to go inside. "I have to get to my locker before class. See you at your truck."

"See you." James absently pulled grass out of his shirt and reached with his mind for threads of his dream. It always vanished the instant before he woke up. The past few nights he hadn't slept well, because he had waited for the dream to come. But always, right before dawn, he would fall into a deep sleep and dream this calling song, and he'd wake without the words.

The bell had rung. James stood up and went back inside.

* * *

Sunday morning James was up early. Granddad came into the kitchen and said, "Pour me a cup, would you?" Grandad liked his coffee thick with cream and sugar. James put it on the table and sat down beside him with his own hot black coffee.

"Your mom called last night after you went to bed," Grandad said. "She told me not to wake you."

James had heard the phone ring, but when he realized it wasn't for him, he ignored the murmur of conversation. "Where is she?"

"She didn't say."

"She never does."

"Doesn't help to be sullen. She is an irresponsible woman, but she is your mother."

"Tell me something I don't know," said James, slurping his coffee.

"The human child is the longest animal in maturing," said Grandad.

"Oh, cut it out."

"I was referring to your mother, although a case could be made for yourself."

"It's probably your fault she's so wild," said James. "You were always away on some field study or dig."

"Is it her fault you're so sensitive?" The corners of Grandad's eyes crinkled with humor, but James was looking into his cup.

"What do you mean?" he asked defensively.

"Case in point," said Grandad. "I can't even talk about you being sensitive without your getting touchy about it. Your mother was just like that; it must be genetic."

This time James heard the laugh in his voice and looked up. "Sure," he said. "Genetic and environmental. In either case it comes directly from you."

"Ridiculous," said Grandad. "I'm never grumpy."

"As a hound dog. Melancholy and moody." James spoke in falsetto: " 'Oh, I'm so old. My aching back. It's going to rain.' It never does, you know."

"What, rain?"

"No, ache," said James.

"How do you know? You don't have to live in this frail old frame. You don't—"

"Moan, moan, moan," said James.

"James." Grandad stopped the teasing. "She really hurts you, doesn't she?"

James didn't respond, but he pulled his hands tight around his cup.

"She hurts me too. Sometimes I'm so proud I almost cry. Like when I hear her songs on the radio. But other times, when I see how she ignores you and takes us for granted, I get so steamed up I do cry."

James didn't know that. He looked up at his grandfather. "You want some more coffee?" he offered.

"I'm glad you're here with me," said Grandad.

"I'll get you your coffee," said James.

CHAPTER IV

By the afternoon of her second day in the women's hut, Spring Rain was bored. Yesterday Raina had come back in the evening and made corn cakes on the hot fire rocks for her. But today everyone in the village had work to keep them busy, except Spring Rain.

She thought about the son she would have, that she should have been. It was going to be difficult for him. If she had been a boy, all would have been simple. She would have learned the old songs, the sacred words and their significance. She would have learned how to listen to the gods and hear their directions. She would have had the understanding. But she was a girl.

In her tribe, it was for the women to hold the land, and the family was carried through the women. But it was the men who worshiped the gods, who worked the magic. The men went into the kivas and held the celebrations and ceremonies. It was forbidden for the women to know the sacred elements. The center knowing, the most holy, was known only by the first ones. Anasan came from those ones who had tested the earth, and the next seer could only be a son of his line.

But the boy would have to learn the words of the songs, and the likelihood was slim that Anasan would be alive long enough to teach his great-grandson. When Spring Rain was young, Anasan thought on this long and hard until he found some sort of solution. She was seven when he approached the village with his reasoning.

He stood on the roof of the tallest house, and the whole village listened.

"Spring Rain is my granddaughter," he said. Spring Rain stood in the shadow of a doorway holding Kyaro who was three and too big to be held.

"My last child died when she gave birth to my only grandchild. The lessons that I would have passed on to my son and he to his son as the future leaders of the village I must now pass on to Spring Rain. The songs must be remembered, and there is no son."

The villagers shifted like loose rocks underfoot. Their voices broke out in protest:

"Our songs passed on to a girl?"

"Impossible!"

"A girl will anger the gods."

"Why not Kyaro? Why not another village boy?"

Anasan answered calmly. "I have fasted many long days and this is clear. The child must have the gift of memory. That gift is in her blood. Our words of power will not go astray in Spring Rain's memory."

The villagers were still angry and suspicious. They had trust in their seer, but perhaps he was too old to have clear thoughts. Grumbling loudly, the men went down into their two kivas, where the men of each clan could go to talk. Anasan came down and walked from one clan to the other, standing firmly by his decision but listening quietly to their complaints.

At last they came to an agreement. Anasan would teach Spring Rain the sacred songs, teach her so well that she could sing them in her sleep. But he would not teach her the meanings. Spring Rain would grow and have a son, and she would teach him all the words of power. Then when the boy knew the songs as well as his mother, he would go on a dream walk. He would fast and sing until the meanings were revealed to him.

This satisfied the villagers, whose trust in the songs would not be broken. And it satisfied Anasan, though he alone knew the complexity of the task for the unborn boy. It would be difficult for his great-grandson to find the meanings, but it would have been impossible without the words. Spring Rain had a memory as clear as fresh water. She would keep the songs well.

Until that point, Spring Rain had lived with Sorsi Raina. When her mother died, she had had a wet nurse, but Raina had been a mother to her. Now, at seven, Spring Rain moved up to the tiny hut high in the cliff to be with Anasan. They began to sing together each morning when they woke up, and again before they went to sleep. They always sang inside Anasan's hut, or out on the ledge when the villagers were too far away to hear.

Spring Rain wondered if they would still sing, now that she was a woman.

Lying alone on her pallet, she sang quietly to herself,

the old power in the words comforting her in the darkness. She wondered about this son she was supposed to have. Where would he come from? She needed to have a man in order to have a son, and all the men in the village were already with a woman. Kyaro was the only one still alone. But this summer just past was only his eleventh. He was much too young to take a woman. He wasn't even interested in trying. If she had to wait for Kyaro, she would be an old woman before she had a child.

What else was possible? Spring Rain sighed and realized that she would have to endure being a woman for a long time before she could break the silence that bound these songs.

By the fifth day, Spring Rain was yearning for a good run. Raina had brought her a pile of yucca spikes, so she could weave a basket. She had to sit in the hard stone doorway in order to get any light.

Late in the afternoon Raina came back. She stepped over Spring Rain's legs and into the hut without saying a word.

"Hey," greeted Spring Rain. "Did you bring something to eat?"

"Feed your own self," snapped Raina, and she lay down on the pallet with her face to the wall. Spring Rain sighed and went back to weaving her basket.

They had never been able to have an easy talk with each other. Ever since Kyaro's birth, there was a space of pain between them. Spring Rain started taking care of the baby while Raina worked. Raina was always busy, so Spring Rain was a big help. When Kyaro was one, she taught him to talk. She held his hands as he learned to walk and run. When he was five, she taught Kyaro how to weave and how to make traps. Raina was his mother, but she mostly left them alone. Spring Rain wouldn't be as lonely for Raina when she was with him.

But now Kyaro was old enough to be useful, and swift enough that he was always sent on errands. Spring Rain found herself pushed into the traditional work of the women instead of out hunting and setting traps with Kyaro.

She had finished another hand's width of her basket. It was going to be a large one, the kind that carried fresh corn up to the village in the cliff from the growing field in the valley. The last two summers hadn't yielded enough to fill even one basket. The plants dried on the stalk before they produced the cobs. The village was surviving on a thin surplus of dried corn from years past and their harvests of prickly pear and nuts. The other plants—the gourds, squash, and beans—were as dry as the corn. What fruit did come was as hard as stone and required cooking in precious water. Spring Rain felt completely empty working on this basket.

When Raina woke up after a while, she apologized for being so sharp. "Well, I was a rattlesnake," she said. "I hope I didn't bite you!"

Spring Rain just said, "Do you feel better now?"

Raina nodded.

"I am glad," said Spring Rain, "because it has been horrible in here, with no one to talk to."

"But I came by to visit you," said Raina.

"There were long times when you were away."

Spring Rain stuck her basket in the corner and sat in the dim light across from Raina. "Are you here for a week now?" she asked.

"I hope to be out for your finishing ceremony."

Here it is, thought Spring Rain. *Here is our time to talk, to get past the everyday chatter and really say something, one woman to another. We're both stuck here, me for another day or so, Raina for a week.* She looked up into Raina's face, hoping to see some warmth of kinship.

Raina noticed her look and started talking quickly about some piece of village gossip. It was as if she were afraid to look Spring Rain in the eyes in case she might really have to say something meaningful.

But the problem that had been pressing the girl for five days now just burst out and interrupted Raina's long story: "Raina," she said, "Anasan said now that I am a woman, I have to bear a son, the one to learn the sacred songs and find the meanings."

Raina was silent for a long time. Her mood change was like a cloud coming across the sun at midday.

"I never understood why Kyaro couldn't be the singer," Raina finally said.

So that was it. Suddenly a lot of things made sense. Raina had never liked it that Spring Rain had moved up to live with Anasan. Spring Rain learned early on that it was useless to try to confide in Raina about the things she was learning from the old man, even those things that weren't bonded in silence. Now she understood: Spring Rain could do something that Raina's own son could not. Someone else's girl she had raised was better than her own born son.

In response, Spring Rain could only repeat the words that had been heard too often. "Anasan says that the way will not be open to anyone but a man from the first ones: those who tested the earth for doneness. So it has been since the beginning. So it is and will be."

"I know all that," said Raina, shaking her head. "But Anasan could teach Kyaro how to listen. . . . Oh, never mind."

She doesn't believe that there is anything special about the singer at all, thought Spring Rain. *She thinks it is all learned. How could she ever understand that the songs themselves have power. That they, not Anasan, choose their voice.*

Her thoughts went back to the problem on her mind. "What I need to know is, how am I supposed to find a man? You have Kawahu for your man, and the next one to be a man in the village is a boy, your son, Kyaro."

"He is not a boy any more than you are still a girl," said Raina defensively. "He'll have his finishing ceremony when you have yours."

"But he is only eleven summers. He thinks the difference between women and men is the way they put their hair."

"Give him time." Raina's stubborn expression broke into a smile. "Maybe, Spring Rain, you will be my daughter after all, if you wait for my son to be your man."

"I will be an old woman before he is old enough for me."

"I always wanted a real daughter."

Her words stung Spring Rain, who still thought of Raina as her mother. "Why don't you have one then?" she said bitterly.

Raina's face clouded over, and her hands went protectively to her belly. She said in a low voice, "Kyaro, when he came out, pulled my living hole apart. He is the only child I will have. And you. You were my girl."

Spring Rain didn't know what to say to that, so she just picked up her basket and wove quick and angry strokes with the fibers.

Raina, oblivious of the pain she'd caused, interrupted her work. "Did you see my turquoise beads? Kawahu brought them back from a trader when he was hunting." She showed the string on her arm to Spring Rain. It was lovely, the rich blue as bright as the sky, with white threads running through the beads like spun clouds. Spring Rain fingered it carefully. She longed for someone to bring her a gift like that; she longed and yet she knew it was as likely as rain.

CHAPTER V

James went up to his room where he'd taken the Anasazi book. As he opened the door, a wave of warm air like a wind off the desert blew into his eyes. His window was open, but it was a calm day. He sat down suddenly on his bed, shaking his head to clear the dizziness. The feeling passed as quickly as it had come, but it left his heart lurching. He recognized the heat. It was the dream again. He woke up this way every morning now with the sun burning his eyes before he had opened them. "What is going on?" he whispered to himself.

James picked up the book and lay down to read. He couldn't concentrate on the words. The dry taste of dust clung to his mouth, and a little fear was caught between his ribs. His room felt claustrophobic even with the window opened as wide as it would go, so he took the book and went downstairs to get a drink of water.

He knew that he had to do something about this project due Tuesday, and he might as well do it on this book, since he had it. Who knew? Maybe he'd get a clue as to what was going on in his life.

In the front of the book, there was a time line:

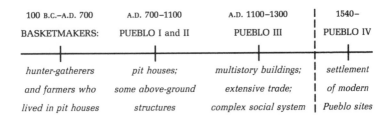

100 B.C.–A.D. 700	A.D. 700–1100	A.D. 1100–1300	1540–
BASKETMAKERS:	PUEBLO I and II	PUEBLO III	PUEBLO IV
hunter-gatherers	*pit houses;*	*multistory buildings;*	*settlement*
and farmers who	*some above-ground*	*extensive trade;*	*of modern*
lived in pit houses	*structures*	*complex social system*	*Pueblo sites*

Anasazi seemed to be a general name for the prehistoric peoples of this area. Their development was labeled in sections. It all made sense until around the year 1300, when the line was broken. After the broken line, the Anasazi disappeared. Any remnants of their culture seemed to be passed down to the modern Pueblo people.

James's forehead felt hot, and he wiped his arm across it. He flipped through the pages to find out where it discussed that break in the line.

He found a chapter with a dramatic title: "The Unsolved Mystery." Apparently, in a rather short period of time, all the culturally sophisticated Anasazi villages were abandoned. Nobody knew why the entire culture vanished. There was a drought that had lasted twenty-six years, and one theory was that the people just dried up. Another thought was that they packed up and went to more fertile lands. Maybe warring tribes from the north came down and massacred them. The Anasazi were a peace-loving people, the book said, and easily could have been taken by surprise.

A hot breath of wind blew across the pages. James

took a sip of the ice water and wiped the sweat from his eyes. He felt as if he couldn't breathe.

All at once, he got fed up. He tossed the book down, made himself a sandwich, and shouted out to Grandad that he'd be back. He was five miles away, enjoying the breeze through his rattletrap pick-up, before it occurred to him that he'd let the book bug him enough that he had to leave the house. He was tired of learning about these people from dry paper. He wanted to see something of theirs, touch something they touched. Something was going on that had a lot to do with them, and he wanted to find out what it was.

He was driving north, toward Blanding, out of habit when it occurred to him. *Of course,* thought James. *There is an Anasazi museum not far from school. I haven't been there since fourth grade.* He got to Blanding, drove on through, and there it was: EDGE OF THE CEDARS.

The building stood out even from a distance. For miles around, there was just a floor of land, broken only by cedar and juniper trees. In the background were the purple hills of Comb Ridge. The red sandstone museum looked as though it grew out of the land. It was a monument to the desert. There were three other cars in the parking lot when James rattled to a stop.

Inside it was dark and cool. James searched through the rooms for something that would strike a chord with his dream. He looked at a lot of things that were interesting, but nothing special. It wasn't until he saw a small pot enclosed in a glass case that he realized what he was looking for. The pot was displayed with a wooden cradleboard and woven yucca sandals. He knew, just from looking at it, that this would hold some answers. The base was simple: smooth white rising to the midpoint of the jar's belly. The top half was painted in an ornate black design. Above, the spiral neck coiled to a lip. James drank in the details. He could imagine the hands as they had formed the pot, smoothed out its curve, and rolled its neck. And then they carefully but firmly drew the lines around and up and down in vibrant, fluid black paint.

It was labeled Pueblo III, c. A.D. 1280. Pueblo III was the group who had lived in the cliffs, then suddenly had left their homes. *That's right*, he thought, *because the last group, Pueblo IV, were living where modern Pueblos live.*

His thoughts were pulled back to the pot. The black design was liquid, running a precise and intricate design over the surface of white clay. The bottom of the pot was so bare in contrast that it felt thirsty: all that luscious painting above, and barren dryness below.

His heart began to beat in his fingertips, and a wave of heat flooded his body. James stopped thinking. He knew he had to spread the ink into the dry half; if he could only open the lines downward into the earth of the clay, its thirst could be relieved. James needed to feel this pot, he needed to touch the black lines and the white clay; he had to try. He felt his hands pull at the lid of the glass case; his eyes were held entranced in the design on the pot. He pulled harder; he jerked at the glass.

Suddenly a piercing siren went off above him. People

ran into the room and grabbed James's arms off the case. Surrounding him, they rushed to the office of the museum and shut the door. The alarm stopped, and in the silence they all erupted with questions at once.

"What do you think you're doing?"

"What's your name?"

"—trying to steal—"

"—no good. They're all marked."

"These things are priceless. You could have broken it!"

"Did someone call the police?"

"What's wrong? Don't you speak English?"

"*¿Hablas inglès?*"

"He's not Mexican; maybe he's Indian."

James rubbed his eyes, trying to clear the picture of the pot from his mind. He looked around at the angry people, seeing their hands wave and their mouths open and shut without listening to their words. There was a heavyset man behind the desk. His face was red through his sun-dark skin. Even his bald head looked hot. He took off his glasses to wipe them with a large handkerchief. He looked up and held James's eyes.

"I need to know your name, young man," he said in a quiet, angry voice.

James tried to think fast, to make up the right answers that would appease these hornets. They were quiet now, waiting for him to answer. He looked at their faces. There were only two other people: a woman with a bright skirt and a toothy necklace, and a younger man wearing a crooked tie and glasses, with big sweat circles underneath his arms. He couldn't think of anything to say. He had no idea why he had pulled at the glass case, and he sure couldn't use his dream as an excuse.

He just crammed his hands into his pockets and said, "My name is James Winter."

They seemed startled to hear such a tone of voice from their juvenile thief. Only the man behind the desk took it without notice, wrote his name down on a pad on his desk, and asked, "Address?"

"Thirty-three Pine Wood Lane, in Bluff," said James.

"Bluff." The man looked up from his pad and pulled off his glasses. "That's where old Charlie Winter lives. You're not related to him, are you?"

Oh, hell, thought James. *They know Grandad. What's Grandad going to say when they tell him that his grandson is a thief. From a museum, of all goddamned places. Grandad's life work was to find things for museums, and here I'm caught trying to steal pottery.*

"I wasn't trying to steal anything," he protested to the three people in the room. "Please don't call my grandfather. I don't know what happened. I just had to hold that pot in my hands." He tried to explain to them about the school project, and reading the book about the Anasazi. He said that he had gone out looking for something that he could touch so he could know what things felt like to them. When he saw the pot, it was the most beautiful thing. . . . He wondered who had made it, and what it felt like. He just had to try to hold it. "I wasn't going to hurt it, I swear!"

He stopped talking when he saw the man behind the desk start to smile. He didn't think what he was saying was very funny, but the man said, "We've got here the makings of a good archaeologist, just like his grandfather." When the other two protested, saying how he could have ruined a priceless artifact, the older man said, "No offspring of Charles Winter would ever hurt an old pot. That old man has more gentleness in his hands than anyone I know."

James left the museum after having been shown the collection room and allowed to handle some broken pots from a new dig. They were nice to hold, but they weren't any big deal. He asked about that special pot, where it had been found, and who had made it. They showed him a huge map stuck with pins for all the sites. The pot was from site 425A5276, a little ruin down in Chinle Wash.

"It's a small, not very exciting site," said Mr. Longrun, the director. "We didn't find much more than these three items. The village was pretty well destroyed. The houses were built on a rock, which broke off, and everything was rubble. These things were tucked away between some large stones long before the avalanche, like someone wanted to keep them safe and come back for them."

James memorized where the site was in relation to the roads he knew. It was way down in the Navajo back country.

When he finally left, the director invited him back to do more research. "Only next time, keep the lids on the cases," he said, clapping James on the back.

When he got out in the bright sunshine, James

breathed in the fresh air and ran to his truck. It started quickly, and he drove away from the museum, away from the city, back down the quiet highway home. What had come over him in there? He wasn't stupid. He knew that all cases in museums are locked; he knew that you couldn't handle museum pieces. But that need to hold the pot had been real. He could have found out something important if he'd held it.

He had a clue, anyway. He knew where the pot was from. Maybe if he could find that ruin, he'd find out what was going on. He felt like he was going crazy. Maybe he was going crazy.

He needed to walk. He pulled off the side of the road and got out of the truck. For a while as he went along, the scene played and replayed in his mind, but slowly it loosened its grip on him and he was able to look around and see where he was.

Way up in the sky he watched a hawk wheeling. It soared gracefully; the clouds piled high as cliffs seemed to brush its wing tips. James looked at the clouds; they were white only on the edges. The center bulged black and moving, and the sky behind them was a bright blue that could crack instantly into rain. The wind, picking up slightly, lifted the edge of James's T-shirt and filled him with exhilaration.

Right then he decided what he would do for his assignment. He would forget the paper part of it. That was all artificial anyway. Instead, he'd take pieces of this landscape home with him and shape a model from it. He could represent the Anasazi cosmos in miniature, trying to design a piece of their daily life. He could show more about them in a model than he ever could in writing.

The air smelled brisk like rain. Quickly he gathered up samples of each tree and bush, of seed pods and small sticks and pebbles that could represent animals. He pulled off his shirt to hold his collection. His empty sandwich bag was stuffed into a pocket of his jeans, and he sifted in small piles of sand, separating each color with a twist. The whole rainbow was in the earth; he knotted off brown, gold, russett, maroon, tan, white, even dark purple and aqua sands.

Folding the corners of his T-shirt together, James raced back to his truck and arrived just as the first few drops spattered the dust on his windshield. He drove home slowly, enjoying the torrential rain.

CHAPTER VI

Come with me, Spring Rain." Raina climbed all the way up to Anasan's hut where Spring Rain was getting ready to sleep. Raina had left the women's hut that morning; she had spent only four days there. But what did Raina want with her this evening? Spring Rain wondered. It was rare for the woman to make the climb to the hut. Spring Rain stood up to go.

They climbed down the ladders in silence. "What is it?" she asked finally as they walked down the path to the desert.

"We are going to get clean," said Raina. "Tonight is the finishing ceremony for you and Kyaro."

Spring Rain walked quietly, noticing the sand shifting over the edge of her sandals and feeling the heat of the day dissipate with the first evening breezes. It was dusk, the time when the night creatures start to cry for their darkness.

"What happens at the ceremony?" she asked quietly.

"Well," Raina answered slowly, as if considering what was appropriate to say, "it is for children to become adults and take their place in the village."

"I know that, but what happens?"

"You meet the gods."

The way Raina said those words sent a chill through Spring Rain. She wanted to ask more, but she knew to respect the gods and their rules for silence.

They stopped in a hollow place between two sand dunes and untied their strings. Even though it was just her summer apron, Spring Rain felt naked without it. Raina looked her over with a critical eye.

"You are certainly changing, aren't you?" she said.

Spring Rain looked down at herself. She hadn't even noticed when her body had started to change from as straight as Kyaro's to rounder like his mother's. But now there was weight at her hips and fullness at her breasts. It was all so new it felt tender, almost painful. She hated Raina to look at her. She squatted down in the sand, picked up a handful, and rubbed her skin until it stung and glowed.

Raina did the same. Then she brought out some leaves of sage and crushed them between her palms with sand. She rubbed the scented mixture on her arms, breasts and belly, and between her legs. Raina gave some to Spring Rain and helped her to perfume herself, but she rubbed too hard. Spring Rain didn't like Raina touching her. She closed her mind and stood still, allowing the powerful smell to fill her head.

"This is what your man will love." Raina's voice came through her thoughts. "When you want him to come to you, rub yourself with sage. The smell makes him very excited."

Spring Rain looked up coldly at the older woman. "I don't have a man," she said.

"Oh, but you will," said Raina, dismissing the obvious, "and when you have him, and he touches you, it feels wonderful."

Raina's voice was so strong it frightened Spring Rain. She pulled on her apron again and walked away, turning her back on the whole conversation.

"Wait, Spring Rain," called Raina. Spring Rain waited but did not turn around. "You have to go to bed right away now that you are clean," Raina said.

"Why?" asked Spring Rain. "Do I get dirty so easily?"

"You just have to. That's all," said Raina. "Perhaps you will dream of your man."

Spring Rain laughed without pleasure, and they walked the rest of the way in silence.

She dreamed she was back in the women's hut, smelling of sage. A strange man came through the door. She could only see his outline because he blocked the light. But he looked young. She tried to tell him that he was not allowed in here, but he kept approaching, his hands reaching out toward her.

"Wake up, Spring Rain, my little one. Wake up." She opened her eyes and realized that it was her grandfather, not some strange man, holding her shoulders. She sat up on her bed, and Anasan handed her a dress, the kind she only wore in winter. It was a deep blue cotton shift that left one shoulder bare. It still smelled of winter smoke. Anasan tied a yellow feather to her hair whorl.

"The time has come," the old man said solemnly, and

his walk was not slow like Spring Rain's, who was just waking up, but light and excited. He climbed down the cliff as if he were a young man and led her to a kiva ladder. She had never been allowed in a kiva before.

There was a red-fire glow coming up out of the hole, and several men were singing a slow song. Spring Rain's heart beat in her ears. They went down into the kiva slowly. The winter dress felt odd against her summer skin.

Anasan took a bowl of pollen from a ledge and stroked yellow stripes on Spring Rain's forehead and cheeks. The men sang a long, slow chant, and Spring Rain leaned back against the kiva wall. Her anticipation waned, and she felt her eyelids start to shut. The singing droned on and on.

She woke with a start. A beat throbbed slowly, then pounded, then whirled faster and faster. It was a dancer on the floor drum; he made the tone-wood sing with his flying feet. Above the fire, the kiva hole had been covered by a black blanket, and the room was filling with smoke. All of a sudden, in the fury of the pounding sound, the blanket was whipped away, and there stood a masked god.

Spring Rain gasped, and heard another. Kyaro and Raina were on the other side of the kiva. Kyaro looked frightened and pale. The god made the drumbeat start up again by pounding his feet on the floor. He danced around the room, his hands and arms moving in ancient symbols.

Spring Rain was frozen. The dancer was both beautiful and awful. The people in the kiva sang to him. She recognized the song and sang with all her voice. The sound grew furious. The dancer's legs and arms flew to their limits in precise movements. Then he held up his hands and clapped out loud. Twice. There was silence.

In a solemn chanting voice, he called Spring Rain by her whole name: "Tamong Yoyoki"—Gentle Rain That Falls in the Spring. She shrunk inside herself and went up to meet him. He commanded that she remove her dress. She shivered even though it was hot in the room. He told Spring Rain to hold her hands together above her head. She did. She had never felt more bare and vulnerable. She yearned to look at her grandfather, or at Kyaro, but she kept her eyes on the horrible mask of the god.

From a rawhide loop at his side, he drew out a pointed yucca switch.

Then with as perfect a movement as the dance, he drew back his arm and whipped the girl, first across one side of her ribs and then across the other. Her eyes stung and she bit her lip hard, but she did not cry out. When he was finished, she walked back to Anasan with her arms still lifted away from the reddening welts.

Anasan put his dry hand on her shoulder for a moment, then helped her on with her dress. They climbed up the ladder and heard the god say, "Kyaro!"

Spring Rain could hear the switch, and it echoed across her own sore ribs. Kyaro was younger, but he still didn't cry out until the end. When it was over, there was silence.

It was painful to lie down on her bed of small twigs

and leaves. It seemed that any way she moved, the stripes across her ribs got poked or scratched. But when she finally got to sleep again, she dreamed of a baby curled in her arms, a baby boy.

CHAPTER VII

James woke up excited. He shook away the thirsty remnants of his dream and smiled. Today he could put together the things he'd brought back from the desert. He sat up in bed, saw his homework on the desk, and remembered it was Monday. "Damn," he muttered, and he flopped back down on the bed. Then, "Forget it. Forget the whole thing." He sat back up. "I'm sick today," he shouted out the door to Grandad.

He had to create the model before tomorrow, and he didn't want to rush through it. If Twitchell was going to accept a model instead of her precious paper, it would have to be really good.

James brought all the stuff down to the kitchen table and laid it out between the breakfast dishes.

"Feverish, I can see," commented Grandad.

After breakfast, James went out to the garage to find something to make his model in, and came back with the large metal basin they used when they were changing oil. It was greasy black inside, but that didn't matter; James would only fill it up with dirt. Out in the garden, he dug up a shovelful of clay, and filled the pan almost to the top. He shaped the clay into a mesa, and cut into the side of the cliff to form an overhang. He got distracted for half an hour painting a watercolor sky on heavy white paper.

James got out the sand, and as carefully as a sand painter, he sifted out layers of colors so they stuck in the wet clay. He planted tiny sprigs of piñon to show vegetation. For water in the canyon bottom, he squeezed his gel toothpaste in a clear blue line and leveled it with a wet knife.

James was in the kitchen all morning. When his grandfather came in for lunch, he inspected the project, picked up a knife, and made a few adjustments to the side of the cliff; it wasn't ridged just right. An hour later they sat down to sandwiches with muddy hands.

James liked his grandad's attitude; he was old enough to know that it was not the end of the world when you missed a day of school. Most kids' parents got too hung up on that. His mom, if she were home, would probably have had a screaming fit if he spent the day making a model instead of going to class. She liked screaming fits. And his dad—he didn't know what his dad would do. His dad probably wouldn't see the value in either school or the model. His dad had gone to reservation school and quit as soon as he could. His dad quit everything as soon as he could.

James picked up the lunch plates and rinsed them off. Way in the distance he could see the Navajo Twins—a pair of buttes that marked the area. He inspected the base of their mesa so he could make his more correct.

No matter how much he did, the model was not as grand as those monolyths. These people, these Anasazi, lived notched into the cliffs. They built their houses in the shape of the mesas. That's all James had left to do, the houses, but they were the most difficult.

He went back to work sculpting tiny clay boxes with fingernail notches for doors and windows, and pine needles for ladders. He worked all afternoon until his back ached and the sun went down.

James was five minutes late when he brought his model into class. He pretended not to notice that people were staring at him.

The class was silent for a minute or two after he sat down. James looked over at the model, on a shelf by the door, and admired the blue-green river and the splendid sunset sky. He felt eyes boring into the side of his head.

"Ahem." Mrs. Twitchell was waiting for him to turn around. Her face was flushed, and she looked mad. James quickly turned around to see what was the problem; she was looking straight at him. He felt naked all of a sudden.

In a very quiet voice, she addressed him. "What is that filthy thing doing in my classroom?"

The class tittered. James looked at the model again. He saw the grease stains on the outside, but they were insignificant when you saw the carefully carved houses and cliffs within. He smiled and stood up. "Let me show you," he said. She would understand as soon as she saw how meticulously it was done. She loved details. "It's my model of an Anasazi village." He brought the model up to her desk.

Mrs. Twitchell clasped her hands behind her back and stared up at the ceiling as if she didn't want to soil her eyes by looking at the pan. "Mr. Winter," she said. "You were absent yesterday. But you haven't been present in my class for the last three weeks. You were supposed to come to class today with a ten-page, typed report, not a piece of junk. I would prefer it if you spent the rest of the year in the library this period. If you expect to pass the course, I'll need that paper—with no muddy fingerprints—by the end of school. You may be excused."

James was stunned. He went back and got his backpack and carefully carried his model out of the room. His face was hot, and he fought to keep the angry tears from spilling out of his eyes. She hadn't even looked at the thing. He spent the rest of the period in his truck.

As soon as he opened the front door, Grandad called him into the living room. When James came in, Grandad looked up from his chair. "I had two phone calls about you today."

From his tone of voice, James knew who they had to have been from. He flushed mad. He had begged Mr. Longrun not to call his grandfather. The other call must have been someone from the school about Mrs. Twitchell. James had meant to tell about what happened in school; he was pretty sure Grandad would understand. But he'd never forgive this museum mess-up!

"Maybe you should tell me what happened," said Grandad.

"Yeah, sure," said James. "Just a second." He went into the kitchen to get himself a glass of Coke, his mind racing. Who was it who had called from school? Mrs. Twitchell herself, or the principal? And how had Longrun explained what happened? He seemed like the type who would leave it up to Grandad to make sure James had learned his lesson. James went back into the living room with his Coke, feeling defenseless.

"That stuff is poison," said Grandad. "I don't know why I let you drink it."

"Because if you didn't, I'd drink it anyway," said James.

"I know," said Grandad. "What happened?"

"Sunday or today?"

"Let's start with Sunday, so I can understand why I had to find out from someone outside the family rather than from you."

"I wasn't ready to tell you."

Grandad's eyes questioned, but he didn't say anything.

"It's to do with my dreams."

"What dreams?"

"Every morning before I wake up, it's like I'm being pulled at in my sleep. My ears are ringing with this weird song that I can never remember. My eyes burn from this bright light. Even if I wake up before dawn, my eyes feel like they've been staring into the sun. And when I try to bring back the picture or the sound, or even what it was all about, my mind blanks out."

"Is this the same dream you were complaining about at breakfast a little while ago?" asked Grandad.

"That was the first time. It comes back every night."

"What did you mean when you said it tugs at you?"

"It pulls, right here." James rubbed the soft spot between his ribs.

Grandad nodded. "So what does all that have to do with the museum?"

James studied his grandfather, trying to decipher how much he already knew. It was impossible. "It's that book, the one on the Anasazi," he said. "When I'm reading that, something weird happens. The feeling of the dream comes back, and . . ." He stopped. "And I still don't understand."

"Go on," said Grandad.

"Well, I went out to the museum because I wanted to try to find something real to connect with the book. I saw a lot of stuff that wasn't too exciting, but then I saw this pot." James paused.

"Ricardo Longrun said you tried to open the case. He said you told him you wanted to feel the pot."

"Yeah. If I could have held it, I would have known something important, I think."

"Okay, that's Sunday. What about today in school?" asked Grandad.

James's throat tightened with anger when he thought about that class. Very quietly he said, "That woman is a—"

"I'm sure she feels the same way about you," said Grandad. "You're quite good at provoking."

"But she wouldn't even look at my model. You know

how good it is, and she wouldn't even look at it!"

"Are you sure you presented it in such a way that she could appreciate your work?"

James was silent.

"So you're out of that class for the rest of the year," Grandad said.

"It's only two weeks," said James. "But I have to sit in the library for the whole time writing a ten-page paper that she'll never even read. She'll just give me a high enough grade so that I'll pass and she'll never have to see me again. She didn't even give me a chance."

Grandad left the room, closing their discussion. James went to the piano and played until he smelled hamburgers frying on the grill. Dinner was quiet; the air was still and fresh like after an electric storm. James felt that somehow Grandad understood more about what was happening to him than he did himself.

CHAPTER VIII

Y ou forgot to smooth the neck," said Kyaro.

"Go away." Spring Rain was tired of being pestered. "I left it that way because I wanted to." She was smoothing off the bowl of the pot with a soft stone, rubbing the clay until it shone. The neck rings were still coiled like a sleeping snake. Kyaro lingered for another moment, but Spring Rain rubbed vigorously and didn't look his way. He gave up and climbed back down to the village.

Spring Rain sat at the end of Anasan's ledge, enjoying the quiet now that Kyaro was gone. It was midday, but the air was cool. It seemed as if the season had changed in the few days since the ceremony. The sun was losing his strength. Sitting here, she could see over the whole village, and way out beyond, across the desert. Smoke from the kivas floated up softly across her view.

She had been here every evening with Anasan, season after season, every night since she was seven. They came here to sing, long and low. They were singing the words of the gods, singing the hero tales. There were no new songs now, but they would sing to remember all the many she'd learned since the first time. Often they would finish their singing and talk together. They'd discuss important things, like how the village had traveled on its three great migrations, and how it would go on the fourth to complete the circle. The fourth journey would take them to the land where the river rushes by the fertile fields.

Their conversation of the night before wrapped around Spring Rain like a blanket. Anasan was telling her about this mesa on which their village was built. It was a mesa layered with lives. People from the beginning of the world had come to live under this cliff, and the spirits of those who had moved on were all still here. Anasan often said that he wanted to die here at the cliff, so he could join the many who still sing in the rock.

"These songs," he said to Spring Rain, "are the songs of all time, of all who came before, and of all who follow after."

Spring Rain asked, "Are the spirits of those who come after also in the cliff?"

It was a strange question, and she didn't understand the answer. Anasan said: "After, when it is here, is the same as now."

Later, when the evening grew still, she asked him for a story. She'd heard it many times before, but she had new reasons for hearing it now. "Anasan," she said, "how did my mother meet my father?"

Her grandfather looked at her a long time. Touching her hand, he began.

"Your mother was the last of my children. I sired three boys and four girls, but your mother alone reached childbearing age. Oh, the grief I have known!"

He stopped talking, and Spring Rain listened to his sadness for a while.

"But your mother, she was the most beautiful and tender. She could listen to the cry of the animals and the whisper of the rock. She could sing to the stars and they would answer.

"When the time came for her finishing ritual, it happened just as it did for you."

Anasan looked into Spring Rain's eyes and smiled. She smiled back, waiting for what she wanted to hear.

"When the ceremony was over, all the young men of the village came, one by one, to ask for her, and to prove their valor and devotion.

"There were many then. These were all boys whom she had run and played with. Your mother cried each night over the decision. She wanted none of them, but she didn't want to disappoint any of them. It was difficult and painful." Anasan was quiet again for a moment.

"One day a stranger walked up our path. He spoke our language roughly, as a learned tongue. He was tall, his skin was rich and dark, and his hair hung in a long tail between his shoulders.

"As my daughter served him his evening meal, he held her eyes with his powerful gaze until her smile split like lightning. While he ate, she stood by my side, and all through the meal he looked our way.

"In the morning, he mounted the ladders and came to

my door. Instead of asking for her, as I fully expected he would, he proposed a contest:

" 'I know a woman as beautiful as your daughter must have many offers,' he said. 'But such a woman should only have the strongest of men. I will join in contest with any of your villagers. We will run a foot race, climb a cliff, throw a spear, and shoot an arrow. If this proves insufficient, we will each spend three days tracking and killing an animal to feast the village. The size, age, and kind of animal will determine the winner.' Those are his words as I remember them," said Anasan.

"And so the contest was set. Your mother watched from up here, both fascinated and afraid. Our young men are known for their speed in running, so that race was tight. The stranger had the advantage of his height for climbing the cliff. Those contests were all close, but the stranger won each one indisputably.

"The village youths were not satisfied. They decided to go out on their own for a three-day hunt—weaponless. This had not been a condition, but since the stranger carried no weapon, our men disdained to as well.

"In three days each came back: one with a rabbit, one with a prairie dog, one with a rattlesnake, and one even had a coyote.

"But when the stranger came back after sunfall, stumbling with weariness, he carried a large antelope buck, sleek and heavy as if sleeping on his shoulders. And when he told how he caught it—running down the buck for two days and a night until the antelope gasped with exhaustion and fell down dead—it was decided that the stranger would be your father, Spring Rain."

"But what happened to him, Anasan? Where did he go?"

Her grandfather was still for a long time. "When you were born, my little one, and your mother died, he was filled with grief. In the village, he had no kiva, no sacred place to go and feel his sorrow. And the villagers, instead of helping him, turned against him, called him the stranger, and blamed him for taking away their Kokoma, the loveliest woman of the village. It was more than that. Without your mother, the line of the seers was broken. All that was left was an old man and an infant girl. What would happen to the wisdom of the village?

"So, one morning, he was gone. He left in the night."

"And that's all?" asked Spring Rain.

"That is all. He is gone from the village, and the villagers have cast him out of their thoughts. He is gone."

They sat quietly for some time, watching a hawk brush the edge of the cliff.

"Do you think he will come back some day?"

"No," Anasan answered slowly. "If he is still living, he has found his journey. That man is a strong one; he is a wanderer."

"What about me?" asked Spring Rain. "Won't he come back to me?"

"I am sure that your father thinks many times about the infant born to the woman-wife he loved."

Then, in the silence of the late evening, her grandfather started to sing: "Aa'na bahnta aa'na ka." With his rawhide hand on her shoulder, they swayed in the still, warm air and made one clear tone, singing two levels. Like the red of the sand and the red of the sunburned sky, they were two with one spirit.

Spring Rain rubbed the clay pot, humming absently to herself. It was a rain song she was humming, and this was a water pot. It all seemed so futile, the songs and the symbols. That is why she left the neck coiled, breaking the tradition of their village's pottery. It didn't help to make them all the same. The rain still didn't come. Maybe something would change if she changed the pot. She didn't believe that; she knew she was being foolish. Only the gods could change the weather. But she was tired of being useless.

Late in the afternoon, she was sitting down with the women when Kyaro came to ask her help with a trap. She gladly wrapped up her work and ran off down the cliff path with him. The trap was set out in the desert.

"I don't know how you can sit with them and chatter all day long like a bunch of sparrows," said Kyaro.

"I don't chatter."

"Well, you sit there and listen to them. That's almost as bad." Kyaro was mad because Spring Rain used to spend a lot more time with him before the finishing ceremony. Now she was expected to be with the other women. She didn't like it any more than he did, but she wasn't going to be called a sparrow!

"I don't even listen to what they say," she said. "I am too busy thinking."

Kyaro didn't answer. They had walked down the mesa path to the desert floor and across to the base of a butte. Kyaro's trap was here, half finished.

54

"I needed another pair of hands," he explained, "and the children can't hold still long enough."

So Spring Rain pulled the trap apart while Kyaro wove in some camouflaging twigs and grasses. Then the trap was finished and set, and they walked away quietly.

"When are you going to check it?" asked Spring Rain.

"In the morning when the birds call, before the sun rises."

"I'll come with you."

"You can't," said Kyaro. "You are a woman. You have to get up with the sun and make the fires."

Spring Rain didn't say anything, but the next morning she was there at the base of the cliff waiting for Kyaro when he came down. He smiled when he saw her. "You're not such a woman after all," he said. Then they were silent. In the trap they found a rabbit—thin and bony, but meat nonetheless. Kyaro was very excited. He wanted to go eat it right away, wanted to build a fire out there in the desert and eat it while the sun rose.

"Don't be foolish," Spring Rain told him. "It has to hang for days before it has any taste. Besides, you know that any meat caught has to be shared with the whole village."

Kyaro picked up the rabbit and tied a carrying thong around its feet. "Sometimes," he said to Spring Rain, "I get so sick of this place. I'd like to just run off and live on my own. I bet that I could find a place that grows better corn than here."

"You probably could," said Spring Rain. "The corn barely even sprouted last spring. We'll be living on reserves again this winter. But even so, you wouldn't be able to live alone in the desert. What about wolves and coyotes who are just as hungry as you? What about water? You know all the land is as dry as dust."

"I know," said Kyaro, "but I still hate to stay here, doing nothing while the old bird women gossip and the men have stopped talking at all."

"Anasan says you won't have too much longer to wait. It is almost time for the fourth migration."

"What is time to Anasan?" asked Kyaro. " 'Almost' could mean when I am a grandfather. I might not live to 'almost.' You know that Anasan is never going to leave this village. He wants to die here with the old spirits. And the village won't go anywhere without a leader. I don't see a leader among us. Where is the male descendant of Anasan? You hardly fit the description.

"Besides," he said, kicking a rock, "I don't believe in those old rules anymore. I think they are decayed, and Anasan has gone sour."

Spring Rain looked at Kyaro with fury and shock. His words scorched her, saying outright the very things she was most afraid of, and this last accusation was inexcusable. "You are so young," she hissed. "You do not know a thing."

"Is that right, little chosen one?" Kyaro sneered. "Well, what did you learn in your finishing ceremony? Did the great god reveal himself to you?"

Spring Rain spoke, trying to scratch him with her voice. "I know more about the gods than you could ever know, boy or not. For I know their words. I know their songs. I may not have the meaning, but their words live in me, and I hold them. You are too young to be playing with doubt. Disbelieve the gods and there will be strife in the village. Our people will starve, our elders will die of thirst, and our babies will fall from the womb."

"Don't you see?" said Kyaro, full of angry tears. "Don't you see that our people die already? And if I don't escape, I may die too!" He ran from her, carrying his rabbit and stumbling in the cool desert sand.

Spring Rain stood there for a moment, crying inwardly for him, then she turned away and went back up to the village. There was a fire to light and corn to grind.

CHAPTER IX

It was eleven o'clock at night, and James couldn't sleep. He was thinking about his mother. He could never figure her out. Sometimes she was warm and sweet; sometimes she treated him as though he didn't exist.

He went downstairs to get himself something to drink. Grandad was sitting at the table.

"Still awake?" James asked.

Grandad nodded. "Cocoa?" he offered.

"Sure." James sat down at the table. "How did they meet?" he asked. "I mean my mom and my dad."

Grandad didn't look surprised at the suddenness of the question. He just filled the cups and sat down next to James.

"How old are you? Seventeen years ago," he said, "your mother was at school in Santa Fe. She went to the gas station and used my credit card. Reading the name, the attendant said, 'Winter? That's part of my name: Wintersun.' I guess they spent a lot of time together, right from the start. When she called home, she said her cold life had been filled with sunshine. She even brought him here once."

"What was he like?" James interrupted.

"Oh," said his grandfather, "young, full of himself. He tried to be mysterious. He said he was the son of a medicine man, so we talked some about Indian mysticism. I was working on West African folklore at the time, and it was interesting to make the comparison."

"Yes, but what did he look like?" asked James. "Do I look like him?"

"The parts that aren't your mother do."

"What parts?" asked James, exasperated. Grandad was always precise when the subject was boring, and vague when it was important.

"Your hair is from him, obviously, and your skin and your cheekbones," said Grandad, "but your eyes and mouth came from your mother. It's odd for you to have green eyes with Indian coloration, but that's how you came out. Your father's eyes were deep dark brown, almost black."

"What kind of Indian was he? Where did he come from?"

"He would never say exactly. He must have been some kind of Pueblo, because he certainly didn't look Navajo. Sally said the name of his village meant Fast Water by the Fertile Field."

"That sounds optimistic. The only fast water around here is the San Juan."

"I think he was from New Mexico. That's where most of the Pueblo Indians live," said Grandad.

"Where is he now?" asked James.

"I don't know."

"When did he leave?"

"When he found out that Sally was pregnant, he disappeared. She told me that she had lost her James Wintersun and gotten her son, James. She lived here for a while, taking care of you and waiting for Wintersun to call. Finally, she went out nights and started singing in a club. Her group got together, and eventually they went on tour. You stayed here with me."

"What about my dad? Didn't he ever ask about me?"

"Here I am," said Grandad with a laugh in his voice, "stuck being father, mother, and grandfather to you, and all you do is ask for another."

"That's not what—" James stopped. His grandfather was teasing him, and he knew it. But still . . . "But still," he said, "I should know about him. I should at least know where he lives and what he does. I should at least know what he looks like."

"That would be next to impossible," said Grandad. "He is long gone."

James sipped his cocoa. It was pretty cold by now. He thought of the map on the wall of the museum, the red pushpin that indicated the ruin. He thought of the pot, almost in his hands. He wanted to go there. It had nothing to do with his father, or did it? His father was an Indian who disappeared before he was born, and he was looking for Indians who had disappeared centuries ago. What difference was time when they were impossible to find?

"Grandad, as soon as school is out, I want to go on a long hike," he said impulsively.

"Alone?"

James nodded. "It's important," he said. "I've got some things to figure out. I want to get out in the open so this dream clears up. I want to understand why my dad left."

"That might not be so easy, your never having met the man."

"I just want to think about it."

"Where would you go?"

"I'd like to try and find that mesa where the pot from the museum was found."

"Isn't it on the Navajo reservation? They don't allow just anybody to walk around."

"It is," said James. "But Rocco can ask his dad for me and it'll be okay."

"You aren't hoping to find yourself a pot, are you? I'm sure they've gone over the area with a fine-tooth comb."

Even the suggestion made James's heart race. What a great idea. "They may have missed something," he said hopefully.

"I'd doubt it. Besides, it's illegal. If you found the place, you wouldn't be able to dig anything up, or take anything."

"Then you'll let me go?"

Grandad rubbed his bushy white hair so it stood on end. James could sense the reluctance.

"You've got to let me go sometime," he said.

Grandad nodded. "It's more than that," he said, but

he didn't say what. Finally he smiled. His clear blue eyes showed how deeply he trusted James. Who needed regular parents anyway? James smiled.

"Time for bed," said Grandad. He rested his hand on James's cheek for a moment.

That night he dreamed he was walking in an Anasazi ruin looking for someone. He looked through low doorways, into dark rooms. He climbed up endless footholds cut in the sandstone walls. Nobody was there. All the rooms were dusty and empty. But something pulled him from room to room. Someone must be there, and James had to find him. Finally James left the rooms and climbed to the top of the cliff. And there it was. He felt something run through his veins like electricity. He looked up and saw two shooting stars burst into a blazing arc through the sky.

The person James was looking for was here. He was standing so close that he could feel skin warmth. But the plateau was vast and barren. Not here, not anywhere for miles around, was there another person to be seen. He was suddenly overwhelmed with the feeling of how small and powerless he was in this universe of a landscape. And then the presence of the other person was gone, as if he had just walked away. He felt sickeningly empty, desperately alone.

"Wait! Where are you?" he called out to the empty sky.

The tears on his pillowcase woke him up, and the feeling of abandonment welled up inside. He didn't remember why he was so upset, but he couldn't stop crying. Then he shook himself and got up and went to the window. It was three A.M. He resisted the urge to go in to Grandad's room, the way he used to do when he was little.

He looked for the familiar formations, one Dipper, then the other, the Pleiades, Cassiopeia. The exercise brought his mind away from his raw feelings. His father left him and his mother left him. His mother didn't even want to talk to him on the phone. James thought of Grandad and felt stronger.

A star fell out of the sky, and suddenly James remembered the dream that had awakened him. The clarity of the image brought goosebumps out on his arms. He left the cool night air and curled up again in his sheets.

In the morning, James woke fresh and glad, with a feeling of excitement in his fingertips. He jumped out of bed and into the shower before he realized what was different. This was the first morning in over two weeks when that plaguing, heat-ridden dream hadn't pushed him awake.

Rubbing a towel on his hair, James poked his head out the door and shouted down to Grandad: "What's for breakfast? I'm starved!"

"Why so chipper, chipmunk?" Grandad shouted back. "Blueberry pancakes. I bought some fresh blueberries just for you."

James whistled bird calls through his teeth as he went to get dressed. Blueberry pancakes for breakfast. Only two more days of school. What a great day.

"Oh, shit!" he said as his toe poked a hole through his

sock. He remembered that he had a ten-page paper to write by tomorrow. He grabbed some lined paper out of a drawer in his desk, folded it, and stuffed it into the pocket of his jeans. He bent over in front of the mirror and finger-combed his hair into place. Satisfied, he went downstairs whistling.

At school, he spent three periods in the library trying to put the paper together. He ended up with a lot of questions, and not much in the way of answers. The librarian gave him a stack of books with sections about the Anasazi, and James took them home that afternoon.

Grandad was asleep in the living room when he got there. James mixed up some lemonade and poured two glasses. He brought one in quietly and set it on the side table near him. Grandad opened his eyes, blinked himself awake, and said, "Oh, it's you, James. I just this moment dropped off."

"Sure you did. You could be asleep for hours and you 'just dropped off.' Have some lemonade."

James gave himself half an hour to relax, play the piano, and talk with Grandad. Then he headed upstairs to work on the paper. Grandad brought his dinner up to him, and he dripped ketchup on two or three pages. He wiped it off with his sleeve and kept on working.

He was finished around midnight, and he put down his pen with a thunk. What a funny sense of freedom. He went downstairs to get himself a glass of milk. Gulping it down, he remembered that the paper was supposed to be typed, and almost choked.

"Goddamn it!" He slammed his hand down on the

counter. He picked up the milk to pour some more when Grandad came in. "You still up?" James asked.

"I've been reading," said Grandad. "Get that paper finished?"

"Yeah," said James, "but I just remembered it's supposed to be typed. She probably won't even accept it."

"That's a problem."

"Grandad, you're such a sage. Can I use your typewriter?"

"No, boy, you go to bed. We'll worry about it in the morning."

"But, Grandad, it's ten whole pages! I can't—"

"I said go to bed. I've typed more than that in my day."

"You mean you'd—"

"You need your sleep, James. So do I," he added as an afterthought. "But I don't have to go to school. What time does it have to be in?"

James realized how exhausted he really was. "Fifth period—one-fifty."

CHAPTER X

Spring Rain's first autumn as a woman had been slow, with little food to harvest. She had avoided the complaining women as much as possible by going out to help Kyaro, but his company wasn't much better. She remembered how they had once sat together on a rock by the empty fields, talking to pass the time.

Kyaro had kicked at the sand. His feet were wrapped in cloth and tied into sandals. "Do you realize," he asked, "that the cold time is coming? My feet are warm now, but in ten days they won't be."

Spring Rain pulled her blanket around her shoulders. It was true; the days were shorter, and the wind blew through her bones as if it were playing a flute.

"So what will we do about it?" Kyaro asked angrily. "Should we just sit back and die like the rest of the people in the village? Spend the whole day sleeping to keep warm? When you're asleep, you can dream about food."

"You could go hunting," suggested Spring Rain, "or weave something."

"Hunting? The animals hide and sleep through the winter, same as the people do."

"We have to eat something!"

"That's the problem," said Kyaro.

"You could weave blankets to keep us warm."

"Old men weave," said Kyaro.

But he had hunted. Spring Rain had helped him to make fresh traps, and every day that winter Kyaro had gone out to set them. He had brought his bow as well, in case something came close. Most days he had come back empty-handed. But when he did bring something back—a gopher or a rabbit, sometimes even a quail—the whole village had come out from their rooms where they huddled for warmth and joined in the tiny feast.

It was warmer when the snow was on the ground. When the sky was covered with clouds like a blanket, it kept in the heat. But some days were clear ice blue with a cold white sun and a wind that could snap you in two like a stick. At least the village, notched into the overhang of the cliff, was protected from the worst.

Four people had died that winter.

Old Atoko had died. Spring Rain had stayed up with Anasan for three days after. She hadn't wanted to be among the loudly mourning women. Atoko had been kind; she had always shared her food, even when she was hungry. Spring Rain had grieved in silence.

When the long cold pulled back and the rocks began to hold some heat again, the slow process of sorting seeds began. Only the large kernels, full of moisture and with a white center flame, were kept for planting. Spring Rain and Kyaro worked side by side. They placed the good seeds carefully on a blanket moistened with precious water. The bad seeds went to the mata for grinding.

"There's not enough here for a second planting if the first gets washed away," said Kyaro.

Spring Rain nodded, picking over the kernels. It was as if each good one held life for the village and each bad one told its defeat.

She watched Kyaro looking so determinedly at each seed. *He's much older having twelve winters,* she thought. *He is still rude, in the way, always playing tricks. But now he is terribly serious sometimes. He feels the burden of the village, and he is not quite strong enough to carry it.*

She wondered what he would be like in a few winters if he were her man. And she shivered. He would gladly come on her and give her a child—from what the women say about their men, Kyaro has all the right qualities: self-centered, eager—but then he would run off and play, and leave her with the pain. Spring Rain remembered Raina's screams when Kyaro was born. She thought of the pain she had to endure each month, alone in the women's hut. Sorsi Raina said that pain was just the beginning of having a child. It got much worse.

And if Kyaro were the father, he would be out hunting a rabbit while Spring Rain screamed. So what, she asked herself, what was so different about Kyaro from all the men in the village? The only other man who had been different was her father. It wasn't talked about, but Spring Rain had heard that he even violated purity and came into the women's hut while Spring Rain was being born. He had heard his woman scream and went inside to hold her. He was with her when she died.

But why isn't he with his daughter now? The question clawed at Spring Rain before she could push it out of her mind. *Why doesn't he care for me? He doesn't even know my name.*

She looked down at the small pile of corn in her hands, and all she saw were weak, fireless seeds and death for the village.

CHAPTER XI

When James got home from school that day, he went into the kitchen. Grandad had set out a pitcher of lemonade with two glasses. "Expecting someone?" asked James.

"You. How was your last day?"

"Great," said James. "It's over."

"What did your teacher think of your paper?"

"I didn't see her. I just left it in her mailbox. Thank you for typing it."

James drank his lemonade and stared out the window without seeing anything. He wanted to leave on his trip as soon as possible. He tried to reconstruct the map in his mind, tried to remember exactly where that red pin was in relation to the roads he'd have to drive.

"Grandad?" he asked. "Do you have any good maps of the area around here?"

Grandad went out to rummage and came back in a few minutes with a couple frayed and ancient geological survey maps and a Utah/Arizona road map.

James laid down the road map first and traced where

he'd have to go. West first, and then south, down U.S. 191. He'd have to turn west again on some road that wasn't marked here. He turned to the survey map and found a couple of possibilities, then started searching the Chinle Wash for ruins. Several sites were marked. He'd have to guess which one was most likely the red pushpin.

"You know, we could just call the museum and find out exactly where the mesa is," Grandad said.

"I thought of that," said James, "but I don't really want them to wonder why I'm going out there. They'll probably feel protective about their special dig, and send someone out to keep an eye on me."

Grandad shrugged his shoulders. "How long are you planning on being gone?"

"I have no idea."

"Well, stay as long as you need. Don't come back because you're worried about me."

The thought that Grandad expected James to worry about him was a real surprise. Grandad was supposed to worry about him, not the other way around. James was the one going on the trip. He knew that Grandad could take care of himself; he had all his life. But he was seventy-four years old. James wondered if he should worry. It sounded like Grandad was a little worried himself. James was annoyed with himself for not having realized this sooner.

"It's okay, Grandad," he finally said. "I'll go do what I have to do, and you stay here and hold down the fort."

Grandad smiled. "Is your camping gear still in the basement from last summer?" he asked.

"Yeah," said James. "I was just going to get it and make sure it's all together."

"What do you want for supper?" asked Grandad. "You probably need to do a bit of shopping, and I thought I'd get something nice for supper while we're out."

"Do we have enough charcoal for the grill?"

"I think so."

"Great! How about barbecued chicken?" James suggested as he went down the stairs to the basement.

James curled up in his covers. It was late; he and Grandad had stayed in the kitchen talking and thinking of things to stuff into James's backpack. It was leaning like a well-fed cat against the bed now. James had rolled up a sleeping bag and tied it on, but he'd decided against the tent. He took a thin tarp of plastic instead. You'll be sorry when it rains, Grandad had said, but James didn't want any more bulk than he already had. He could always find some sort of shelter, or tie the tarp between some trees. He stuck in a line of rope.

He'd been camping out on his own before. He usually took several trips by himself every summer, and each year he and Grandad went up to the mountains in Colorado to camp and fish for a week. But this was the first time he was planning on being away for a long time. Actually, he had no idea how long the trip would last, or where he would stay, but he was prepared to spend at least a week on his own without needing anything.

Still, the pack was pretty small. He didn't load up on

any gear other than food and jugs of water. The water was going to be heavy, but worth it. He lay in bed with his head propped up so he could see out the window, and tried to think of what he'd forgotten. Mosquito repellent. He rolled over and made himself breathe slowly so he'd relax and go to sleep.

In the morning, Grandad already had the batter made, so James poured on a waffle and slipped out the back door. He was back again in a minute with a handful of marigolds, which he set in a small bowl of water on the table. The waffle was done, and James and his grandfather split it, using the real maple syrup instead of their usual raspberry jam.

"Did you have that dream again?" Grandad asked.

James nodded.

"I thought so. You look a little tired still." James didn't answer. He just brought another waffle to the table and buttered it, preoccupied.

"So you're heading off today," said Grandad.

"I won't be gone that long. I'll probably be back in a week or two."

"Maybe not."

"Don't be so mournful," said James.

"Realistic," said Grandad. "I want to ask you to write or call at least once a week, but I'm not sure how often you'll come across a phone or post office."

"Grandad! I'm not going to Mars," said James. "If you don't hear from me, it's probably because I'm a lousy writer, especially if I get involved with something. I never write Mom."

"Nor she you."

"But don't go calling the police if you don't hear from me."

"So when do you recommend I call the police?" asked Grandad.

James looked up quickly. "I'm sorry, Grandad. I didn't mean . . . I mean, nothing will happen. I'm not going so far away. I'll be okay."

"I see," said Grandad. "In other words, I'm to use my discretion when calling the police. If I feel it in my bones that you're hurt and lost, I'll call. As long as I feel that you're okay, I'll just wait. Are you sure you trust my bones? Will you get that waffle? It smells burned."

James went for the waffle and said, "You've got good bones."

CHAPTER XII

Kyaro was right. Something had to be done. When the seeds had been planted sixteen days ago, the earth was so dry it had to be pierced with a sharp stone. Now the seeds needed water. Each day without rain would mean another plant that would not sprout. It was a long wait.

Kyaro went about his work those days with his head down, seeing no one. Spring Rain tried to talk to him, but he didn't answer. He spent more and more time in the kiva. Spring Rain wondered if he had his belief back again and was trying to reach the gods by his attention.

Kyaro was trying to change things in any way that he could. The only place of power open to him was the kiva. But Spring Rain had the songs. Even without willing them, the words pressed at her voice to be sung. She woke each morning with wild and painful music pounding in her head.

One spring morning, so early it was still black, the songs were loud enough to wake her up. She knew what she had to do. She had to wake the sun with her singing, to ask him to bring along clouds. She thought of where she could sing to the sun, and not to people. There was only one place where people never went: the top of the mesa. The climb was too difficult. But Spring Rain knew a way.

A narrow track led up the cliff from the roof of Anasan's hut. At the end of the track was a crack, almost invisible from below, that was large enough to admit a small person. A massive slab of rock, as big as the cliff itself, leaned up against the mesa wall, fitting tightly except for this chink. It made a small triangular cave that Spring Rain used to play in when she was younger. Now she only went there when she needed to be alone.

Beyond the cave, if she climbed like a spider, she could get up to the top of the cliff. This was where Spring Rain went now, just making out the fingerholds by the clear light of the moon. She was carefully unaware of the sheer drop below her.

Just before the top there was a ledge, enclosed on three sides. The roof was open to the sky. The walls held back the wind, and Spring Rain stopped there for a minute to chaff her cold hands.

The sky was no longer black; the stars were paling and the rim was almost colorless. *The sun is going to rise,* she thought, and she climbed swiftly up to the top. The songs were ringing in her ears, ready to sing in the sun; ready to sing for clouds to cover the sky like thick clumps of clay and squeeze out a gentle rain on the land. The songs were going to sing in a son to learn the mysteries of the words and lead the village to the land of fast water and fertile fields.

Spring Rain stood straight on the eastern edge of the

mesa and sang those majestic songs of power out loud. One after another, she sang without pause. Not understanding the words, she had no idea whether they were the right songs to please the gods, but she had to hope. The sun rose over her singing like heat from a fire, and the day dawned warm and dry.

Every morning after that day, the songs would press her from sleep and she would go. Every day she would sing to the morning sun, to ask him to dim his brightness with clouds. But every day the earth grew drier. If the sun were to take the earth in both hands and shake it, she was sure it would rattle like a dry gourd.

Then one day, when Spring Rain got to the top of the cliff, she could not sing. There had been a small breeze from the east that morning so she lifted her face, enjoying the air as it fingered her skin. It was early, still dark when she got there. She rested on the hard, packed sand and watched the sky. All of a sudden, two shooting stars blazed through the sky. The Twins, she thought, the twin gods have sent a sign. She was awed into silence, and just sat at the edge of the cliff without singing as the light melted across the sky.

Suddenly she felt a person standing next to her: A knee poked her back, and a hand brushed over her head. She whirled around, afraid. The mesa top was empty. But someone was there, someone was listening, searching. Had her songs found a listener? Was it waiting now for her song? She couldn't sing; she had no voice.

She stood up carefully, trying not to shake. Quietly, not stirring a piece of dust, she backed across the mesa to where her path led down. Slowly, quietly, she lowered herself to the ledge. Hidden from view, she scrambled down as fast as she'd ever climbed to the room between the rocks. She watched the sunlight reaching a thin finger into the crack of stone and waited for her breath and her heart to steady. Then she let herself think about what had happened.

There had been a presence there, but no body. She had a sense that it had come to hear her song. She was afraid of what the songs were truly asking for. These were powerful words that spoke for themselves. Whom had they called, and who had come? Spring Rain knew what she meant by singing, and the songs all but forced themselves out of her. But she would never know what she was really saying when she sang the ancient songs.

Now it was late. She had to get down to the village, or the women would start asking questions.

That night, Kyaro cornered her as she was on her way up to Anasan's house to go to sleep. He looked full of himself; Spring Rain smelled trouble.

"What do you do with yourself before the sun comes up?" He closed his eyes to narrow slits as if he were trying to look inside her thoughts.

Spring Rain gave him her innocent look and shrugged her shoulders. "Sleep," she said. "What do you do?" She turned to climb up the ladder, but Kyaro blocked the way.

"Let me up," she said. "I want to go to my bed."

"Not until you tell me what you do."

"Why is it so important to you?" she asked, and she

sat down to wait until Kyaro got tired of asking.

"Do you meet someone?" he asked.

She said nothing.

"How could you? There's no one to meet," he said. "Or is there?" He tried to catch her off guard.

It didn't work.

"Do you go to your little cave?" he asked.

Spring Rain looked up, surprised.

"Oh, yes," said Kyaro, "I know all about that cave. I followed you there a long time ago."

"You sneaky piece of rotten meat!" hissed Spring Rain. "Why don't you mind your own business?"

But that had given Kyaro an idea. "You know," he said, "I could always follow you again."

"You wouldn't dare," said Spring Rain.

"Nothing could stop me," he said, "except, of course, if you told me."

Spring Rain's eyes snapped with frustration.

"Come up to the ledge so no one can hear us," she said.

"What about Anasan?"

"He is already asleep," said Spring Rain, "and besides, his ears are not very strong anymore. He would never be able to hear us if we sit at the top of the stone steps and talk quietly."

Kyaro thought that was fine. He was still young enough to love a mystery. Maybe that was why he was being so inquisitive. She followed him up the cliff to the ledge.

"Well," said Kyaro expectantly as she sat next to him. They swung their feet over the edge.

Spring Rain tried to sound as mild as possible. "I go to the top of the cliff to sing."

"The top of the cliff?" Kyaro was amazed. "How do you get up there? No one goes there."

Spring Rain was relieved. If he didn't know this much about her secret place, he didn't know much at all. "It is a very difficult climb," she said, "and only I know where the toeholds are. No one else has been up that way."

"What do you mean, sing?" asked Kyaro.

"Just that," said Spring Rain. "I sing the songs that Anasan gave me."

Kyaro gave her a troubled look. "Can you do that?" he asked. "I mean, is it safe?"

Spring Rain nodded. She didn't trust her voice to say yes.

"But who do you sing them to?" asked Kyaro.

Spring Rain was quiet for a long time. At last she said, "At first I sang them to the dark sky and the new sun." She paused. "But something has been listening."

"What do you mean, something?" asked Kyaro eagerly.

"I don't know. I have never seen it."

"A spirit?" asked Kyaro.

"I don't know," said Spring Rain.

They were both quiet for a long time then. The air between them almost crackled with thoughts.

Finally Kyaro spoke again. "What do you ask for when you sing?"

She looked at him closely. He wouldn't understand if

she said she asked for rain for the seeds in her womb as well as rain for the seeds in the earth. So she answered him simply.

"Rain," she said.

CHAPTER XIII

James drove along an empty highway with the wind blowing briskly across the cab, taking the whistle out of his lips. He had a road map laid open on the seat, pinned down with an old pair of tennis shoes. He needed to go south until he was in the Indian reservation area, then branch off the highway onto one of the smaller roads where he could start looking.

Being alone and away from his everyday routine, James was able to think about the last few weeks. The daily dreams he couldn't remember; the pot and its insistence on being held; the way the Anasazi paper wrote so fluently; his grandfather's unquestioning acceptance of this trip. It was as if his ordinary boring life were being blown in a specific direction by a strong wind.

He was on the reservation, almost at the Arizona border. Up ahead a road branched off and out across the desert. He checked the survey map and it looked like a possibility. He decided to take it.

It was a dirt road, well graded at first but still slow. He enjoyed the sense of peace that comes from being the only person around for miles. The sky was filled with cumulus clouds, and the blue far beyond those billowing white cliffs was as bright as polished turquoise. James leaned forward, resting his chin over the steering wheel and just gazed up at the sky, dizzy with the color of the fresh air.

With a loud hiss, the view filled up with an explosion of hot steam. James slammed on the brakes and turned off the ignition. Jumping out, he stood a few feet away from the old truck and watched it spout steam like a geyser. A few minutes later, it was all over. James went over to inspect the damage.

A hose to the radiator was blown, and the radiator was bone dry. Even if James put in all the water from his jugs, it wouldn't do any good without a new hose.

He climbed back into the cab to think.

There was no way he could drive anywhere, period. He could walk the ten miles or so back to 191; he cringed at the thought of a dusty walk all that way in this heat. Besides, he hadn't seen another car on that road the whole time. It wasn't as if it were a major highway. *Well,* thought James, *this is what I'm here for. The truck's not going anywhere, and I said I wanted to do some exploring.*

He put on his backpack and walked off down the road. The sandwich he'd had at home was long since gone, but he knew he shouldn't dig into his pack for a picnic yet. So he just walked, and hummed a bit.

After a while James got out an apple. He hadn't checked his watch when he left the truck, but it was four o'clock now.

After another hour he ate half of a sandwich, drank a swig of water, and trudged on. He watched with considerable enjoyment as the sun began to sink behind a mesa on the horizon. The mesa had a peculiar shape. From where he was standing, it looked as if something had taken a bite out of the side. The desert below the mesa was drenched in shadow, but the sky was still pale blue and bright, glowing orange only in the clouds. He probably had another hour and a half before it would be completely dark.

Maybe that is the one, thought James, and he stepped off the road and started hiking through sand and brush, leaving civilization behind.

He was more cheerful now. It was as if he had left all his responsibility back there with the road. The past few weeks had been rather taut; that fight in the museum, and all the mess with Twitchell. James felt as if he'd escaped it for the first time. He remembered a song Grandad had taught him when he was a little boy—a walking song:

> *I love to go a-wandering*
> *Along the mountain track*
> *And as I go I love to sing*
> *With a knapsack on my back. . . .*

It was senseless, but fun, and James felt as free as he had when he was five; only now he appreciated it.

He found a place to camp between two juniper bushes where the ground was soft with sand. He rolled out his sleeping bag and built up some rocks for a fireplace. Light and easy without his pack, he went off to find some wood.

He had brought hot dogs for the first night, and he had to eat them all so they wouldn't go bad. He found a branch with twigs poking out like fingers and roasted all five at once. They tasted magnificent.

James sat up for a long while, watching the fire burn itself out. Finally, too tired to keep his eyes open, he climbed into his sleeping bag, running his hands over the top of it first to make sure no rattler had crawled in to spend the night with him.

He wasn't exactly up with the sun, but the day wasn't hot yet when James had put his breakfast and sleeping bag into his pack and set out across the desert toward the mesa. He'd come around a bit, and there was no longer a gap on the edge, but the mesa itself was still intriguing. He'd had another dream. He could remember bits and pieces, for a change. This mesa was in it, that much was clear. And there was a person too. He remembered a feeling of longing, like loneliness, or wanting someone to love you. And like all his dreams in the past month, there had been a song. This time the tune— an eerie, chordless melody—was just on the fringes of memory. He tried unsuccessfully to sing it. He sounded like a wild animal in heat, he told himself. Good thing there was no one around to hear.

The mesa stayed in the distance for the first couple

of hours, then all of a sudden the ground dropped off and James could see the whole thing. It was huge; James was surprised by its size. The flat top towered above and became a jagged silhouette as James came under the shadow of the cliff. When he was actually next to the wall, James peeled off his backpack and set out to explore.

He wanted to find the place where the cliff cut in, so he walked off in that direction. As he rounded the end of the mesa, a pile of fallen rock blocked his path. He scrambled up to the top of the pile, and could see the edge of the hole from where he stood.

The top of the cave curved in as smoothly as the outline of an egg. The curve started toward the front again, then broke off in a sheer slice, as if the egg had been cracked lengthwise and the shell was the scree pile, crumbled here at his feet.

James looked down at the rocks he was standing on. He noticed that many of them had flat, regular edges. He bent down and picked one up. It was not quite a foot square, maybe four inches thick. "This looks like a brick," he whispered. He set the rock down gently and climbed over the pile looking for more. He found fifteen perfect bricks, and many broken pieces. "Are these from houses? Do you suppose this could be it?" he whispered to himself. He sat back on a flat rock and stared up into the hole, trying to imagine a village built into this huge cliff.

He saw, as if materializing for his imagination, a ruin of a small hut, still standing, way up in the top of the cave. It rested on a tiny ledge, as precarious as a wild-flower growing on a boulder. James sucked in his breath. He had to get up there, to run his fingers over those bricks. But there was a cliff as smooth as sandpaper between the house and him. For a long time he sat there, gazing at the hut and wondering what it had been like living there, and what had happened to the people.

Finally he got so hungry that he had to go back to his pack. After lunch he spent several hours sitting in front of the cave with his notebook drawing pictures of houses set in a cliff, trying to guess what it must have looked like when people lived there. When the light began to slant across his page, throwing his work into shadow, he decided he'd better quit and find a place to camp. His back was leaning against the cliff, and he thought he might climb up to the top and spend the night up there. He stepped away a few feet and gazed up. It would be incredible. He would be able to see for miles.

The cliff was way too steep where he was, so he put on his pack and walked around, away from the ruins, until he found a place that was eroded enough not to be vertical. If he climbed in long zigzags instead of straight up, it shouldn't be too hard.

In some places it was a scramble; James had to fasten the waist belt of his backpack and use his hands. It felt like the pack was trying to pull him backward off the rock, but he drew his shoulders forward and climbed eagerly. All of the tiredness from the long walk evaporated, and he attacked the hill with the exuberance of a kid, and laughed at the thought of it.

The hardest part was the top fifteen feet. The slight incline straightened off and James had to judge each handhold carefully. It was almost completely dark. Many of the stars were out, but the moon had not yet risen, and James could hardly see where to put his feet. He slipped and scraped his knuckles, and the blood tickled him. "You dumb shit," he said, "why are you doing this?" He had to take a deep breath to stop his tired knees from shaking like a sewing machine. He didn't like the thought of falling down the cliff. No one would find him for weeks. So he carefully looked up and found a place to wedge his aching fingertips, held tight, and scuffled his feet up. Pieces of sandstone broke off under his boots, and when he finally got his elbows up on the top, with his legs still dangling down, he was almost too beat to pull himself up. He lay on the top of the mesa panting, then stood up and whooped.

He was starving, so he found a sandy patch, spread out his sleeping bag, and opened his pack. When he had finished his meal, he cleaned his teeth with an apple. It was dark and windy; he was warm enough sitting in his sleeping bag, but he wasn't sleepy. The stars were piercingly bright in the south, but clouds were blowing down from the north. He got out his plastic tarp and wrapped up his sleeping bag. He fell asleep trying to remember the dream song.

It was raining lightly just before dawn and he woke up enough to pull the plastic around him more tightly. The song from his dream was singing right through his ears. He turned to where the sound was coming from, and in the faint light saw his dream. A naked girl was singing that song to the sky. Her arms were upraised, her black hair fell down her back, and her singing was beautiful, joyous. *What a great dream,* he thought as he curled up and went back to sleep.

CHAPTER XIV

Anasan snored. Spring Rain felt as if she had been awake all night. The air was dry, her throat was parched. She wanted a drink of water, and water to give to her grandfather so he would stop snoring. It was too early to go to the top of the cliff, but she was tired of lying in bed thinking about herself. So she stood up quietly, taking her blanket with her.

She climbed straight up, through her rock room and up to the ledge. There she paused, wrapped in her blanket against the chill. She looked at the stars, still bright in the night sky, and found the deer and the hunter, and the snake that swept halfway across the sky. A star shot out like an arrow from the hunter. *Good,* she thought. *Things will be different today.* She stood up and unwrapped her hair, then climbed over the lip of the mesa and crossed to the eastern edge.

The night was black, but the sky was so close, the stars were in her hair. Spring Rain lifted up her fingers to try and touch them, letting her blanket fall to the ground. She felt the earth through the soles of her feet, she felt the stars through the tips of her fingers, she felt the songs from the center of her spirit come singing through her lips.

As the sky paled with the beginning of morning, its light was softened by a rising cloud, pulled up like a blanket over the head of the sun. The cloud spread quickly over the earth, and Spring Rain, with her hands raised up to catch them, felt raindrops fall gently on her skin. "Weialala leia!" she sang out in jubilation.

She heard a crackling noise behind her, and she turned around and saw a man in a wrapper. Rain in her hair and a man on the cliff top: two things that were impossible. Nobody ever came up here except Spring Rain. Nobody knew the way.

When Spring Rain was sure the man was sleeping, she went closer. The rain fell softly on her skin and she was chilled and wet. His blanket was shiny, like water. What if he was no man? She was suddenly afraid. Quietly she ran back to her ledge to hide. Once she was safe behind the rock, she stood on her toes to look across the mesa at him.

No man had come up her path; she would have noticed. And there was no other way up the cliff. Was he a spirit then, who flew up here? Do spirits sleep? Did he bring the rain with him?

Spring Rain looked up at the sky, and its water splashed in her eyes. She turned from the strange man and climbed back down to the village. Everybody would be out collecting rainwater, and she would be missed. She scurried down, almost slipping. She had never climbed when the rock was wet.

Crawling through her cave a thought stopped her short. Could she have summoned him here with her song? The thought terrified her.

It was time to talk to Anasan. This whole thing was beyond her control now. Why did she ever think that she could do something, that she had to do something by singing? But it rains now, she said to herself as she went into the hut.

Anasan was still asleep. It shocked her that he could sleep while it was raining. Of course, the villagers expected her to be up here with him and to wake him. She shook her grandfather gently. Some of the rainwater dripped off her skin and onto his face. "Ai la la," he said. "What is this wonder, this dream?"

Spring Rain shook him again, spilling more drops. "Wake up, Kwa'a! It is raining."

His eyes sprung open. "I am awake," he said. "I have been awake for a long time. I am just thinking deep thoughts."

Spring Rain laughed at him with her smile. "Did you hear what I said? It is raining, the soft she-rain."

He touched the wetness of her skin with disbelief in his eyes. "What are you saying?" he asked. "There is no rain in the sky. I have looked, and seen only dryness season after season." Then he sat up on his pallet and looked stern and angry. "Is this in fun? Have you spent good water on fun?" He touched her wet hair.

Spring Rain stopped smiling. "Come now," she said. "No games." She helped him up and walked with him out to the ledge.

A curtain of cool rain hung fresh and falling in front

of the overhanging cliff, leaving the homes and people dry, but watering the fields and plants in the valley below.

"Weialala leia!" Anasan cried out. "Weialala leia!"

The people in the village turned to look up at him and lifted their arms in joyful acknowledgment. They were busily setting pot after pot under the streaming gentle rain.

Spring Rain laughed out loud. Then she remembered this morning, how she sang and the rain covered the sun, and the spirit man came to the cliff top. She pulled on Anasan's hand. "Kwa'a," she said, "I think I know why the rain is here."

"What is that?" he asked. "Sing, girl, sing!"

"Anasan, I know why the rain has come," she shouted.

He stopped his singing and looked down at her seriously. "Tell me," he said, "what do you know?"

CHAPTER XV

When James woke up later that morning, the rain was just beginning to let up. He had a fresh, relaxed feeling that comes from spending the night outside on your own in the rain—and not getting too wet. He checked to see if the plastic tarp had let any leaks in. There were a couple of drips, but nothing serious.

He rolled over on his back and stretched. The sky was clearing, the sun was out, and the earth was steaming like a hot tub. Ooh, his muscles were sore, but the scrape on his hand wasn't too bad. He climbed out, pulled on his shorts, and shook out his bag and tarp. He wondered what time it was. According to the sun, it already was midmorning. He must have been pretty tired after that hike.

James was just taking out breakfast when he noticed an Indian girl looking over the top of the mesa. At the same instant, he remembered the dream he'd had early that morning when it'd started to rain, with a girl like her singing the dream song. Maybe she'd know something. Maybe she'd have some answers.

She stared at him without coming all the way up. She looked wild. She also looked frightened, so James stopped staring at her. He just gathered some wood for the fire, and when it was going, poured a little water into his metal cup and set it to heat. When it boiled, he added some instant oatmeal and a little dried milk and stirred it up. Sometime, while he was busy, the girl climbed over the edge and crouched at a distance to watch him. She was almost naked. James looked away and tried to pretend that he didn't notice. Halfway through his meal, he found himself wondering if she were hungry. So he left the cup near the fire and walked down the length of the mesa.

When he was far enough away, he looked back. She had the cup in her hands. She must have eaten the oatmeal, because she was turning the cup over and peering at it as if she'd never seen one. Even though she had hardly any clothes on, she made no attempt to cover her small, pretty breasts. James turned his face away again, trying to figure out where she could have come from. He waited a bit longer, then, moving slowly, he made his way back to the campsite. She was going through his backpack, no doubt looking for more food; but she didn't touch the bags of dried fruit and meat, or even the apples and oranges.

James was near now, and she looked up. She had sharp, high cheekbones, and deep brown skin. Her hair must have been terribly long; it was wrapped in loops over her ears. She looked more Indian than anyone James had ever seen. He reached down to pick up an orange that had rolled on the ground. He peeled it and held out a juicy section to her. As an example, he ate a piece. With a suspicious squint, she put the orange piece between her lips and bit. Her eyebrows burst upward in surprise, and she pressed the whole piece in her mouth. Juice squirted out; she caught it and carefully licked each finger.

James gave her most of the orange, just to watch her face as she ate it. She had incredible eyes. She looked younger than James, but tougher, invulnerable somehow. Her skin was tight along the bones of her face and shone in the sunlight. Her nose was long and narrow, and quite pretty, but it was her eyes that were surprising. They were beautiful liquid black with lashes so dark they looked like painted rings. *So this is the singer,* thought James. *This is my dream come to life. Where does she come from? What is she doing on the top of a mesa in the middle of nowhere? Where is her family? They must be pretty poor, and seeing how she is dressed, very traditional. But they're not Navajo—no Navajos are that primitive.* James listened to the thoughts in his head and decided he was going crazy. He wanted to touch her. He shook himself. Even though they hadn't spoken one word to each other, he already knew that he wanted to be with this girl more than he'd wanted anybody in his whole life. He didn't even know her name. He felt insane.

The girl stood up as if to go. James put the orange peel into his pack and stood up beside her. "My truck busted its water hose," he said. "Do you have a car, or even a horse at your place?" Her face was blank. He realized how absurd his requests must sound to someone from such an old-fashioned family.

Looking hard at him, at his hair, his face, his clothes, and at his pack, the girl finally jerked her head over to the edge of the cliff, as if to say, "Follow me." James shouldered his pack and went after her.

She led him to a semi-enclosed ledge just below the top of the cliff. There wasn't very much room, but the girl sat down easily. James wasn't as comfortable. There was a sheer drop to the ground from the front of the shelter. They looked out at the sky. The clouds, having spent their rain, were skuttling away. It was easier to look at the sky. He was too close to the girl. She smelled funny, and she was so naked. But she was acting as if she were also afraid to look at him, and there was nothing wrong with the way he looked.

After a while, she gave James a long, careful look. She stared at his shorts and T-shirt, touching the fabric with her eyes. Then she pulled her shoulders down and smiled.

James stared at her mouth, then turned away. He'd never seen anyone with teeth in such bad shape. They were all chipped and yellow. It looked as if she hadn't brushed in a month, or ever. He looked up again, at her eyes this time, and smiled back involuntarily. "You don't speak English, do you?" he asked.

She wrinkled her eyebrows at him and said a string of incomprehensible words.

"What kind of Indian are you?" he asked. Then it occurred to him, and the thought almost knocked him off the cliff. What if she was an Anasazi Indian, hundreds of years out of her time. What if his dream had come alive? *Now I really am losing it,* he thought. *How would she ever have gotten here?*

She pointed at herself as if to indicate, "Me?" and James nodded. So she wiped out a clear space on the ground. She drew a circle in the sand and divided it into four sections. In the top left-hand segment, she drew a line across the bottom, and three dots just below the line. In the top right, she drew the same thing, but vertical lines rose up from the dots, breaking through the ground line. In the bottom right corner, she drew the same picture, but filled out the branches so they looked like leaves.

"I get it," said James. "It's a plant!"

She looked up at him curiously and drew the fourth picture. It showed the leaves drooping and what looked like corn cobs sticking up straight and ripe. Then she pointed to the first picture, with just the seeds in the ground, rubbed her arms, and shivered.

"Winter," said James, and pointing to the rest, "spring, summer, fall."

She looked to make sure he understood, then carefully rubbed out three quarters of the picture, leaving only the segment of spring. She pointed to the picture and to herself. For a moment James thought she was spring, or the goddess of spring; but he laughed at the thought, and she smiled back at him when he laughed. "Tamong," she said.

"Is that your name?" asked James. "Tamong?" He pointed to her. She smiled and held up her hand to wait.

Again she drew on the ground. This time it was easy. There was the line for earth, and above it was a cloud. She made the cloud black by drawing quick zigzags across it, and then drew lines of dots down from the cloud to the earth. "Yoyoki," she said. She pointed to the first picture, of Spring, then to the picture of Rain, then to herself, and she said, "Tamong Yoyoki."

"Tamong Yoyoki," said James, "Spring Rain."

"Sprie Ray," she repeated, and laughed at the sound.

"My name is James," he said, pointing to himself. "James."

"Jays," she said.

"Mm," said James, "James."

"Jams," said Spring Rain.

James smiled. Spring Rain pointed to her pictures and to James. What does his name mean?

James shrugged his shoulders. "My first name doesn't mean anything, but my last name is Winter." He redrew the segment with the seeds below the ground.

"Tomo," said Spring Rain.

"How did you get here?" James asked. And when Spring Rain gave him a questioning look, he shook his head. "Forget it, you'd never be able to tell me." He imagined drawing a time machine in the dust, and laughed at the thought.

"Jams?" Spring Rain was pointing again at the picture for rain. She drew a picture of the sun, and a house, and some corn plants. Making sure she had his attention, she brushed away the rain and the corn.

"You had a dry spring?" asked James, pointing to the crossed-out rain, and to the spring segment. His grandfather's garden was growing pretty well, and for spring in the Southwest, there had been quite a lot of rain this year.

"Hey, are you thirsty?" he asked. Spring Rain didn't understand, so he brought out his jug and offered her a swig. She smelled the water, then dipped her two fingers in and drew her tongue along the wetness.

She said something that sounded like a thank-you in her language.

James said, "Have some more." But she shook her head. James was thirsty now that the water was out, so he took a mouthful and screwed back on the cap. Wiping his lips, he saw Spring Rain's look of astonishment. Had she expected him to drink a drip off his fingers as she had? Not likely, he thought. He'd go easy on it, but not like that.

She was drawing again. She put a few more squares by the house so that it became a village. Then beside the village she drew five corn plants—their field. Above this she drew another sun.

James was intrigued. "Is this village your home?" he asked, and he pointed, as she had, down the side of the cliff.

"Hom?" she asked.

"Home," said James, nodding.

"Ray?" asked Spring Rain, drawing a quick cloud with drops coming down from it.

James smiled. She was quick. "Rain," he said.

"Rayn—'ka,' " she said, wiping out the rain and shaking her head.

"No rain?" asked James.

"Rayn, 'ka,' no rayn," said Spring Rain.

"For how long?" asked James, and he redrew the circle of the seasons. "No rain all spring?" he asked, pointing at the spring quarter.

Excitedly, Spring Rain ran her finger around and around the circle, nine times, then to clarify, she said, "No rayn spreen, spreen, spreen," and each time she drew a mark in the sand.

"No shit," said James.

"No rayn," said Spring Rain.

"Yeah, yeah, I know," said James, "and for nine years. You're saying you've had a drought since you were a little kid. No wonder you wanted to leave."

"Jams rayn?" Spring Rain pointed to James.

"Does it rain here?" asked James. "Yeah, it did this year. Yes, James rain."

"Jams rayn, rayn, rayn," sang Spring Rain happily.

Satisfied now that she'd made her point, she reached over to finger James's shirt. It was an ordinary T-shirt with no decoration, just slightly faded turquoise blue. Spring Rain held the cloth like an expert, feeling it between her fingers. She raised her eyebrows. As if to return the favor, she held out her arm for James to inspect the bracelet she wore. It was a strand of small white shells with two round turquoise beads at the center. It looked ancient. She held it up to compare the color of her beads with his shirt. His was a little brighter, but the beads were real. James fingered the stones; they were smooth, not perfectly round, with a grain of white running through the blue.

Most girls wore jewelry that was gaudy and flashy

and looked out of place. But this bracelet was right on her arm the way the gold band looked right on his grandfather's finger. It was as if the roughness of the stones and shells belonged with the dusty brownness of her skin. James smiled at her and said, "It's really pretty." Spring Rain seemed to understand. She fingered the beads, watching James's face.

The sun had reached the top of the cave now, heating up the small space just as fast as the light overtook the shade. Spring Rain touched James on the shoulder to get his attention, then pointed to her bare chest and the blanket she had taken off. James looked away, quickly. Jesus, he thought, what was she doing?

Spring Rain reached for his T-shirt, giving it a slight tug upward trying to pull it off.

"Wait a minute," James said. "I don't even know you. I can't just— What are you trying to do?"

Spring Rain sighed, said something rude, and cleared a space in the sand. She drew a large sun, pointed to the picture and to the sky, and said what sounded like, "You idiot, the sun is up, and it's going to be hot."

"Right, okay," said James, "but just my shirt." He folded it on top of her blanket. Spring Rain stared at his shorts, but James shook his head. "No way. You can wear what you want, but this is what I wear when it's hot."

She shook her head. James looked more closely at what she was wearing. It was a small apron, hand-woven from coarse brown yarn, with fringe on the bottom. The fringe looked like that Rastafarian hair style, with the tangled braids all hanging down. He picked up the blanket that she had left on the ground. It was roughly woven with downy feathers stuck in between the threads. It was dirty and scratchy, but felt warm, hot as a matter of fact. He folded it carefully and laid it back down. He couldn't figure out what was going on. Who was she? What did she want from him? Why was she here?

Spring Rain stood up, talking to him and motioning for him to stay where he was. "Sure, no problem," he said, nodding his head. Then she left. He watched how she climbed down from the ledge across the cliff and into a split in the rocks, about thirty feet below.

The ledge got hotter and hotter, and James grew worried about Spring Rain. Somehow he felt responsible. Would she freak out when she saw where she was? Or maybe he was waiting for nothing. Maybe she had already slipped back to her own time.

He went down the way she had gone. It was a tricky climb. He had to grip with two sets of toes and one set of fingers while the other went exploring for a new hold. It was a good thing he wasn't wearing his boots.

Finally, shaking, he made it to the crack. It was a small triangular cave with an opening at the other end. The relief of coming into the shade was immense. It was so cool! James leaned against the wall for a minute to catch his breath, then crawled across to the other end. This room was comfortable for sitting in, but wasn't meant for standing up. He looked out the opening to see where it led.

Down below, in a huge natural cave, was an Indian village. A group of houses perched together, single-story huts in a half ring in the front. The row behind had some double-high houses, and the back ones went three stories up. There were people all over, most of them wearing just what Spring Rain had been wearing. The kids were plain naked. There were dogs running with the little kids, smoke and ladders drifting out of the roof holes. It looked just like his Anasazi diorama, but much more . . . alive.

James thought of the cave he'd explored yesterday. The single hut, set above all the others, was right here, twenty-five feet below the crevice where he was hidden. But this was a village, not rubble. He moved back into the cave and rubbed his eyes with his hands. His brain refused to function. All he could think was, *It's like the dream. It's just the same as that dream.*

CHAPTER XVI

Spring Rain went straight to Anasan. He was sitting on his ledge with the pot of water that she had brought up to him. He'd had to solve several arguments that morning over custody of water and was quiet now, looking out across the desert. When he saw Spring Rain approach, he said, "See, mooyi, how the desert opens up in flower when it rains. So will you open up with child."

How could you know? wondered Spring Rain. But out loud she chose to say nothing, and instead looked out at the desert with him. It was true; the whole scape was green and flowered, bright cactus blooms and fresh green shoots. Today would be a day for collecting blossoms for sweet soup. This kind of day almost never came.

Her news was so important it pressed out now. "The man is still there," she said, bringing his attention around with a snap.

"Tell me of him," said Anasan.

"I am sure he is not from this land," she said. "His clothing, his speech, his possessions, his eyes . . ." She had a vivid image of those distant but friendly eyes, the color of cactus.

"Not of this land?" asked her grandfather. "Be careful what you say, even to me."

She nodded slowly. "He brought the rain with him when he came," she said. "His clothing—it is cloth of the gods. No person could have woven such fine work."

"What else did you notice?" asked Anasan.

"His name is Jams—such a strange name, and when I asked him of its meaning, he said it had none." Spring Rain described how she had drawn the picture and explained her name to the stranger.

"So we have a visitor," said Anasan. "We will have to be hospitable. He will sleep with me, of course."

Spring Rain was surprised. There were only two places to sleep in Anasan's hut, and one was hers. "But what about me?" she asked.

"You will have to find another place for this short while. Perhaps Sorsi Raina will take you in."

Spring Rain was reluctant to give up her own bed above the village, but she nodded obediently to her grandfather.

CHAPTER XVII

Spring Rain found him in the triangular cave. James was sitting with his back against the cool rock. He'd tucked his T-shirt into his shorts pocket. Apparently that wasn't good enough for Spring Rain. She held out a loin cloth like her own for him to put on.

The fabric itched like chicken wire. He tied the strings in a clumsy knot. There was a flap in the front and the back. He felt obscene. "Okay," he said to Spring Rain, "you can turn around now."

She turned, inspected him, and covered a flash smile with her hand.

"What is it now?" he asked, annoyed.

She pointed to the side of his rear end, touching his skin.

James whacked her hand away. "Cut it out!" he said.

She pointed again, keeping her distance this time, and he twisted around to look. "Oh brother," he said, "my tan line." The place that his shorts cover up all summer long was white as soap. Spring Rain was laughing again. She picked up some red dirt from the floor of the chamber and started to rub it in.

"I'll do that," said James.

It was passable, the red dust. At least he didn't look like he had white war paint painted on his ass. He had a cramp in his neck and shoulders from stooping over in the low room. "Let's get going," he said to Spring Rain, jerking his head toward the village. She led the way.

Past the narrow opening there was an indistinguishable path that Spring Rain skipped down. James followed more carefully. When he looked up behind him, he saw a piece of bright sky and against it, the silhouetted edge of the mesa. In front of him, Spring Rain paused every now and then to let James catch up. She was dwarfed by the walls of rock, like a mouse in a cathedral.

From here he really could feel the weight and protection of the heavy rock ceiling. There were people down there working, and kids playing on the plaza, and all of them were shaded by the arched cliff. The path led down onto the roof of the one cliff house set high above the rest.

The two of them stood on the rooftop and scanned the village, then Spring Rain went over to where a ladder rested and climbed down. James stayed on the roof. He wasn't ready to meet these people yet. He sat, leaning his shoulder against the rock wall, his feet swinging off the roof, and looked carefully down at the village.

It was a picture-perfect museum piece, with all the

extras the museum experts forget to put in, like that man standing at the front wall, lifting his apron and taking a leak over the edge. James smiled to himself.

He tried to think, but it was as if his mind was stuck. He couldn't bring himself to ask the question, and he sure couldn't come up with an acceptable answer. So he let his thoughts roam and watched the village. Spring Rain was beneath him, talking to someone in the hut. He could hear her voice.

This house was like a crow's nest for the village. It was as if there had been a small square of rock they could build on, so they built, without thinking how anti-social it was to be perched up here.

It looked as if the roofs of the houses were used as an extra room. They were piled with blankets and pots, and as many people were on the roofs as were in the square below. The plaza was filled with children and large birds and a couple of dogs. James could see two openings in the floor of the plaza with ladders sticking up out of them. He figured that these must be the kivas. Smoke was drifting up out of one of them. Along the front of the plaza was another retaining wall that looked a little more sturdy than the one up here. The cliff dropped down fifty feet or so before it reached the desert floor.

Spring Rain came out of the house below him and called up, "Jams!" He stood up quickly, brushing off his dusted butt, then looked around to make sure the color was still there. The ladder down was primitive, but it held him. The entrance to the hut was a small, low door, and he had to stoop to get in. The room was pitch black and filled with the smell of a strong tobacco. James felt slightly sick from the smoke and the closeness of the small room. He reached up the wall to the ceiling before he stood up, to make sure there was room.

"Harumh," came an old voice from the back of the room.

"Jams," said Spring Rain, taking his hand and bringing him to the old man who sat in the far corner. "Anasan."

James squatted down on his heels and took the old man's hands.

"Jummus," said Anasan. His voice had a deep lilt.

"Anasan," said James.

They let go of their hands. James had the strong feeling that he'd met someone of immense importance. Strange, because he was just an old man squatting on the dirt floor of his hut.

James's eyes were adjusted by now, and he sat cross-legged in front of Anasan, taking in details. Anasan leaned back against the wall looking at James. His old mouth was a long, strong line between his sunken cheeks. His eyes, what James could see of them, were night black, glinting slightly from the light coming in the door. His hair was thin and gray, sifting past his face, down his back. His shoulders were thin. The top of his collarbone stuck out of the dry skin like a finger poking up from under the sheet. His chest was ribbed; the skin over his stomach was folded in deep wrinkles. The loin cloth he wore was ratty and limp. His knees were balls on top of thin, sticklike legs. And yet, and yet . . .

There was more strength in this one man than in anyone James had ever met. The old man reminded James of Grandad so strongly, he almost cried.

Why was he here, sitting in front of a grandfather, but not his own. How on earth—how in heaven was he ever going to get back home?

Anasan had turned to Spring Rain and was questioning her. Spring Rain hummed a tune for him. It was the morning song, the song he woke up to.

Anasan put his hand on James's arm. He asked James a question. James nodded. If Anasan was asking if he knew this song, he sure did. Anasan and Spring Rain spoke for a few more minutes, then Spring Rain stood to go.

Anasan came to the doorway to watch them leave. James followed Spring Rain along the ledge. When they got to the end, Spring Rain didn't hesitate. She climbed down with such grace that James looked again for a ladder. The only thing there was a line of small holes pecked into the stone.

His toes clung to the rock, his hands jammed into the holes above. James knew this was basic rock climbing, but he wished he had a rope. He inched carefully down the wall, searching for and testing each foothold. He heard a laugh and looked down to see Spring Rain giggling at him.

"It's not funny!" he snapped, and she pulled her face straight. It wasn't that he was afraid of heights; he just felt so naked clinging to the holes in this wall. Spring Rain had a full view of his private parts from where she stood. If he'd been climbing like this at home, at least he'd have been dressed decently.

He was relieved to reach the ladder propped up against the wall and felt like a fool when he finally stepped down onto the roof. Spring Rain came up to him, took his hand, and pulled him over to the ladder down to the next level. All the villagers stopped what they were doing and looked up at the two of them on the rooftop. James noticed two men and a woman walk away from the cluster around the base of the ladder, talking angrily among themselves and staring up at James.

"Hey, Spring Rain," he said, "tell them I didn't ask to come here." But instead of being sympathetic, she shook her head, put her hand over her mouth, and looked sternly at him. *Well,* he thought, *I guess I'd better shut up.*

They sat on the edge of the roof and let the people stare. Some shouted up questions at Spring Rain. The only word he recognized was part of her name, "Yoyoki," and he couldn't figure out if they were talking to her or about the rain that morning. When the crowd started to break away, the two of them went down the last ladder. A few people went up to James, asking him questions with a loud voice as if he were deaf. He stayed quiet and let Spring Rain answer. When she got fed up, she motioned for James to follow her down the ladder. Several people fingered his skin as they went through the crowd, but Spring Rain led him away quickly.

They went into a little room where she picked up a basket. James only got a fleeting impression of the room, small and dark, like Anasan's hut. He wouldn't want to live here. Spring Rain brought James across the plaza and down a steep path to the desert. After the rain, the usually monochrome landscape had turned bright with color. All the red dust had been washed off and delicate desert flowers were bursting out all over the place.

Apparently this was what they had come here for. Spring Rain showed him how to pluck off the blossoms and collect them in the basket. They worked together, walking back and forth across the sand until it was too hot to move any longer. James was so hungry he thought he might pass out, so he was relieved when they turned back to the shaded village.

He followed Spring Rain and the flowers to where a group of women sat working and chattering. They were grinding meal between a slab and a stone. The women looked up when Spring Rain and James arrived and their conversation stopped short. Several of them glared at James. Spring Rain took up a place on the end and set to plucking off the stems. James watched for a minute, then picked up a flower to help.

Spring Rain grinned at him and moved over to give him room. The other women stopped to watch, and pretty soon they were mocking his clumsy efforts. He must look absurd; his fingers weren't used to doing this kind of work. It wasn't easy either. He kept on ripping pieces of the petals.

When they were finished with the basketful, Spring

Rain got some of the corn from one of the women and set to grinding. There was a rapid conversation going on that didn't sound all happy. They kept asking Spring Rain questions, and she gave only scant answers. Finally one of the women, a younger one, pretty and proud looking, brushed off her ground corn into a small bowl and stood up. Shaking her finger at Spring Rain, she said some loud things and took off across the plaza. Spring Rain looked uncomfortable, and James felt like an alien. How could Spring Rain possibly answer questions about him? She had no idea where he came from or what he was like. And if they were asking the purpose of his visit, which was an obvious question, what could she say: He has no purpose; he's here by accident. He doesn't know how he got here, or how he'll get back? That would do a fat lot of good in a village where food is scarce and a stranger is looked on as an extra mouth.

"Jams?" Spring Rain was there, but the other women had left. James must have dropped off to sleep in the drone of their conversation. He had been dreaming about Grandad. They were sitting at the kitchen table together, talking. Grandad had been crying.

He felt peculiar opening his eyes to Spring Rain, with her whole senseless village around her. She held out a pouch, and he took it. It was leather, roughly stitched together. Inside the small opening was corn flour. Spring Rain pointed to him to show that it was the flour he had helped to make. She tied the bag onto his waistband by a leather thong. He was terribly aware of how close she was to him; her skin almost touched his. He thought she hesitated before she drew back again, but he wasn't sure.

"Yoyoki, Yoyoki!" A shrill voice burst in between them.

"Kyaro," said Spring Rain, in an exasperated voice.

He defended himself eloquently, and Spring Rain had to introduce them. "Jams, Kyaro." James looked up at the small boy; he looked around eight, but he could easily be older.

"Karo," James said, "good to meet you. I'm James."

"Jams." Spring Rain nodded.

"James," said Kyaro, showing Spring Rain the right way to say his name. She looked annoyed. Then he said, "Kyaro—K-yaro."

"Kyaro," said James, more correctly. The boy smiled. His eyelids creased at the corners and gave him a perky, impish look. He twisted around on his heel and came down, *chunk,* next to James. He looked at the older boy in a conspiring way and pulled a leather bag off his belt. James knew that look. It was a 'how-much-can-I-bleed-this-sucker-for?' look. James took his guard.

Out of the bag came bone pieces that looked a little like dominoes. Kyaro laid them out and went to find some pebbles. Coming back with a handful, he gave ten to James and kept ten for himself. Spring Rain collected her own. Kyaro stood on one foot and drew a circle in the dirt with his big toe. He carefully set up the pieces, all pointing out from the center.

Then all three of them stood outside the circle and tried to move the bone pieces by casting the pebbles at them in turn. It was fun. James got better as he began to understand how the bone moved around. If you landed a pebble just right, the bone would flip up and over. Kyaro was really good at this. Spring Rain wasn't half bad, but James was thrilled when he got it once.

They'd been playing awhile when someone called Spring Rain away. She handed her pebbles to James and ran off.

Kyaro grinned and squatted down, his toes just on the edge of the circle. James did the same. This was getting serious. They both threw with great deliberation, trying to strike the highest number and get them to move. Both boys yelled out enthusiastically in their own language.

That night James watched one of the women cooking. Her stone stove was hot from the fire. She mixed a little of the fresh water with corn meal, then dipped her fingers in the batter and lightly ran them on the stove. The bread cooked paper thin, and she rolled it up with one hand while spreading the next circle of batter with the other. Seeing James there, she got angry and shouted at him. He left, his stomach growling. Spring Rain brought him some food later. *Primitive tortillas,* he thought. One was spread with bean paste. They weren't very filling, but they tasted great.

The sky was turning violet at the edges. Spring Rain motioned for James to follow her, and she climbed up the ladders to the footholds in the cliff, then scrambled up to Anasan's walkway.

"I don't think this is such a good idea," James said up to her. "I'm not used to this. I can hardly see now, and I won't be able to see a thing coming down when it's dark."

Spring Rain laughed and told him to stop being chicken, or something similar, and James said, "Okay, but you have to catch me when I fall." James climbed. It was easier going up than down, even in the half-dark. Spring Rain waited at the top with a taunting look that said: "See, it wasn't that bad!"

"That's not the part I was worried about," said James. Spring Rain didn't listen to his complaining. She just went along the ledge to Anasan's door, and James had to follow her.

Inside, Anasan sat in the same place. Spring Rain had brought up a packet of dinner for him. Anasan spoke to her in his slow, melodic voice. James listened hard and recognized one word: his name, pronounced "Jumms," with a long, level stare at him. Spring Rain answered him quietly; then Anasan stood up, using the walls to pull himself up. He leaned on to Spring Rain's arm and walked past James out the doorway.

On the ledge, Anasan stood straight. He lifted up his deep voice and threw it across the high arched cave. The perpetual drone of the village froze for a moment, and everyone came out to the plaza to listen. His speech went on for a few minutes, pausing here and there to draw out a word.

When he was finished, the people were still for a minute. Only when Anasan turned to go did groups break away, talking loudly.

Spring Rain and James followed Anasan into the hut. The old man ate his dinner and lay down in silence. Spring Rain showed James a pile of dry grass with a rush mat laid on top. James sat on it, and Spring Rain

117

brought over a blanket. Then she reached down, touched his cheek, and left.

James lay down on the mat and pulled the blanket over him. The grass prickled, and the woven cover poked, and the blanket was itchier than wool. He missed his sleeping bag and he wanted his T-shirt. He rubbed his foot against the hair on his other leg and thought about Spring Rain. All those things he had said to her, all day long, and she hadn't understood a word. But still it felt as if they somehow knew each other. He tried to make his cheek re-feel how her hand had touched him. He even brought his fingers up to brush the place, but the sensation was lost. So he tried to remember the sound of the words she had spoken. When at last he fell asleep, it was dark and dreamless.

CHAPTER XVIII

Spring Rain went straight down to Raina's. She wanted to make up a bed and be by herself for a few minutes. Kyaro was in his corner, sprawled out, sound asleep. Spring Rain thought over what Anasan had said when she brought James up to her bed.

"He is the one. Jumms." Anasan's voice had surprised her as they came in the entranceway.

"How do you know, Grandfather?"

"He comes to a new people and does as they do, without asking questions or challenging. A man from his seed would be able to lead our tribe among strange people and live with them without threatening their traditions."

"He doesn't question because he can't speak," said Spring Rain.

Anasan had ignored her. He stood up and walked out on the ledge. "My people!" He had lifted his voice so it resounded in the high, arched cave. The people in the village stopped what they were doing and came out to the plaza to listen.

"A stranger has come among us." He waited for the echo to die away.

"He brings the blessings of the gods.

"He comes with the soft she-rain.

"He will live peacefully among us.

"We will give him food for his hunger.

"We will give him water for his thirst.

"We will give him a bed for his rest.

"He will live among us.

"He comes with the blessings of the gods."

Anasan turned his back on the silence of the village and went inside his hut. Only then had the village stirred, and like the swarming of bees, their angry voices rose in the air.

Spring Rain had just ignored the sound and showed James her bed. His tender skin was not used to this kind of sleeping; he flinched as he sat down. He lay down, and she pulled her woven turkey feather blanket over him. He had looked like a child, afraid and alone.

Spring Rain pulled Raina's blanket around herself and wished she were up there to comfort him. She missed her own bed, but more, she felt a tender longing for this stranger.

Raina and her man came in, interrupting her thoughts. They were talking loudly about James.

"He spent his entire day with Spring Rain," said Raina. "Hung around her like a rope. As if he has the right to walk into the village one day and claim our only young woman as his own."

Spring Rain wanted to shout out from where she was

lying. But she just lay there listening, angry as the deep red embers of a slow fire.

Raina's man protested mildly, "But he did bring the rain. Is it right to criticize him who brought the gentle rain?"

"You farmer! All you think of are your crops. Have you no feeling for the family line, for the life of our son?"

"He needs food to live," he said simply.

"Besides," snapped Raina, "I don't believe that stranger brought the rain. I think the rain came and he claimed it."

That was it. That stick made the flame. Here they were, discussing her and Kyaro and James as if they were the stick puppets that children play with. They had no respect for Anasan and his words of support for James. And they had no grasp whatsoever of the deep power that brought both James and the rain.

She stood up in the small room. "You may talk all you want behind my back." Her words snapped with fury. "But when the subject is me, I would ask that you hold your tongue while I am in the room," and she stalked outside, taking her blanket with her.

See what your anger will do, she thought to herself. *Now where will you sleep?* She stood for a moment, alone in the moonlight in the courtyard. There was light and activity in the kivas, but everywhere else was silent. She looked up at Anasan's dark hut where James was sleeping in her bed. What about her rock room up the cliff, she thought. She could sleep there. It wouldn't be the first time she'd slept on rock.

So she climbed up the ladders to Anasan's ledge and silently went along and up to his roof. In her chamber she found James's clothing, so she folded it up and placed the bundle under her head to soften the rock.

Her smoking, angry thoughts settled down after a while, and she was able to relax. She thought of James, with his smiling, eager face ready to try anything, even her work. She wondered if he had known that he was coming here. Where did he come from? She felt his clothing under her head. In fact, with the loin cloth on, if you didn't see his eyes or that silly piece of white bottom, he looked like an ordinary young man. Well, not quite ordinary, certainly not from this village.

He seemed a little older than she was, though not much. He kept staring at her breasts, which meant he was more aware than Kyaro of the difference between men and women. But he was so awkward, stumbling. He didn't know what to do with himself.

She went to sleep thinking about his soft hands. They weren't caked with dust and cracked with dryness. His hands were smooth and thin and long like fingers of rain.

CHAPTER XIX

In the morning, James felt someone touching his shoulder. He was sound asleep. He grumbled, "Just a minute, Grandad," and rolled over. But his bed poked him in the ribs as if it were made of sticks, and he opened his eyes to a girl. He closed his eyes again, remembering. This was far worse than that dream. She shook him again, so he sat up and went with her out of the hut, rubbing sleep from his eyes and checking to see that his loin cloth covered him up. The sun wasn't quite up yet. *It's awfully early,* he thought.

They sat up on Anasan's roof and watched the sleeping village. They sat close to each other because it was cold in the early morning. The picture of the cave of ruins he had discovered the day before yesterday came into his mind—was it only then? And superimposed over that picture was this cave with its homes and its people. They were a matched set, today's alive and active, yesterday's crumbled in death. Somehow the living one was more frightening.

Spring Rain leaned forward, brushing her side against

his. His thoughts broke apart; he felt his skin tighten with energy. He lifted his hand and ran his finger down her back, just to feel her warmth. She turned to look at him.

"I'm hungry," James said, breaking the mood, "and dying of thirst. Is there any way I could get a drink of water?" He poked at his mouth and stomach. It seemed that she understood what he was trying to say, but she just shook her head.

"I know!" he said. "I've got a couple of apples up in my pack." His hands reminded her of the shape, and he took a bite out of an imaginary apple. "Why don't we go get them?"

They climbed up to the room in the rock, and Spring Rain went on alone from there, taking James's clothes up with her. In a few minutes she was down, an apple in hand. She raised her eyes in question, but gave it to James. He took a huge bite, and the juice squirted and dripped down his chin, so she decided it was all right to do the same. It was wonderful.

"Spring Rain," said James with his mouth full, "how did I get here?"

"Jams," said Spring Rain in her own language, "where do you really come from?"

It was so frustrating not to have any conversation that James just kept talking. When he paused, Spring Rain would say something. He couldn't understand a word she was saying, although he listened to the sounds carefully. He was sure she couldn't understand him at all either. But it felt good to talk.

"Grandad is going to worry about me," said James. "I wonder what his bones are saying."

"I told them you're from far away and your words are of another family. That is why you don't understand us."

"How long am I here for, Spring Rain?" She turned to him, hearing her name. James asked, "How do I get back home?"

Spring Rain took his hand for a moment and looked in his green eyes. "Somebody said that maybe you came from the angry people in the north. That you come here to learn our secrets and then slaughter us. Do you understand me?"

James heard the direct question, and he looked at her not knowing which way to nod.

"Spring Rain," he said, "I need to tell you about something that happened to me before I came here."

"Jams, you are not one of the angry people, and you are not from any village near here," Spring Rain said slowly. "I know, because you came to me. If you were one of them, you would have come across the land, from the north. You were on the top of the mesa. There is no way to the top other than the way I go, and you could not have come up that way without alerting the whole village. Unless you are a spider who climbs walls, you came by the song."

"Every morning," said James, "for the last three weeks or so, I'd wake up, just dreaming, and not remember it. But you know, it felt like that dream was a high-pitched ringing in my ears all day."

"You come from a strange place," said Spring Rain. "You come to me alone. I will not tell the people of your belongings, or they would run you out as an evil one. They do not like strangers or strangeness. They do not like you already. They would have killed you but for what Anasan said. I am grateful they still listen to Anasan.

"I told them you were naked when you came, like a man who runs long distances until the clothes drop off his tired body. But you had clothes and food-drink. These balls of sharp, sweet food, so wet, so full of taste. Surely you are magic come to me."

James heard the gentle rhythm of her words quiet down and turned toward her. Her eyes were waiting for his look. She was so strange, and yet her whole expression was open with trust. The girls at school all looked caged, as if their tight clothes and makeup held in any person that was there. But here was a girl, as good as naked, sitting with him and still being open and unself-conscious.

He looked at her, and, overwhelmingly, like the memory of a bitter smell, the scent of his dream filled his breath, and suddenly he was sure. Spring Rain was in the dream. She was in that pot, and in the desert, and in the books. It was of her home that he'd built a model; it was her life he'd tried to describe in his paper. It was she, this Spring Rain, who had haunted him night and day for three weeks. Goosebumps ran up his arms and down his spine.

"Did you know that?" he asked. "Did you know me

before I came here? Did you know that you were my dream that I couldn't remember?"

"Jams," she said, "I have something to tell you. My name is Spring Rain. My mother's clan gave me this name as an offering, so I would be a reminder to the gods to bring the sweet rain in the spring. When I was young, the rain still came, but for the last nine springs, she has not fallen. Summer after spring only the strongest plants survive. Harvest after harvest we gather in only enough to coat our tongue for another winter. The plants die of thirst, and the weak among us die of hunger.

James listened quietly, hearing the shape of a story in her words. He thought of Grandad, who sometimes went on and on retelling a memory, until James would listen to the voice, but not the words.

"So one day I took all the songs old Anasan had given me and left my bed, where you sleep now, while it was dark. Everybody still slept. I climbed up the mesa to where you were yesterday morning. There, on the top, I sang. Day after day I sang all the words I know. I hoped some of them would come together to have meaning for the gods. But each morning, day after day, I only called the sun, and he came when I called. . . ."

Spring Rain's voice was lovely; the vowels and catches in the words sounded as natural as a mockingbird's song. It was funny how it felt like they were having a conversation.

". . . in the middle of the song I felt something, like someone was watching me—" she broke off and looked at James "—it was you. You touched me, but I couldn't see you." Spring Rain held James's arm and stared at him.

And James felt the strength of her recognition and knew that she'd remembered him, that his dreams had been her dreams as well.

The moment passed, and Spring Rain went on with her story. "So, you understand, I had to tell Anasan. It was my secret, but then something had happened, and it is for Anasan to interpret these things. And do you know what he told me? He said wait and see. He told me to go back with the women and grind corn and wait. I was so angry, but he laughed and said, 'Go now.'

"So I went. But early one morning, when I was up on the cliff, I finished my singing and you were there." Spring Rain put her hand on the small of James's back and leaned her head up against his shoulder. James felt his cheeks burn, and he closed his eyes. But when he looked again, Spring Rain was still there, so beautiful. His ears pounded; he could hardly breathe, but he took her face in both his hands and kissed her.

Then he held her head against his shoulder and, after all that talking, they were quiet. The heat of the day was rising in the earth, but there was a different warmth between them. Spring Rain started humming softly, and the familiar sound gave James an odd feeling of being in both places at once. If he closed his eyes, he could believe he was asleep in his own bed. But this was real. . . . Was this real? Here was Spring Rain, a real girl, warm in his arms; her hair scratched his shoulder. This was no dream.

Spring Rain and James came back down from the cave and found Anasan standing in the doorway. He made an odd, angular shape, the oddness exaggerated by the lack of clothing. James thought of his own grandfather and wanted desperately to make this scene normal. He almost asked the old man for a cup of coffee."Pour me a cup too, would you, Grandad," he wanted to say, but he didn't think the man would enjoy the joke. "Good morning," he said instead, politely.

Anasan looked at him and smiled. "Gur manik," he imitated the English. And then he said something that sounded very profound in his own tongue. James didn't know how to respond to that, so he just nodded his head to Anasan and turned to look at Spring Rain. She was laughing at him. It was awful to have spent the night in the same room with someone and not even be able to say good morning so he understood.

The village was already active. Little kids were running around in a circle on top of a kiva and screaming the rhyme of a game. Several women were grinding corn, and one lady was chasing after a turkey. Most of the men weren't there. Maybe they were in the kivas, or out working somewhere. He decided not to go with Spring Rain when she went down; he was feeling a bit like a lost puppy, trailing after her all day long. He was glad to see Kyaro scampering up the ladders.

Kyaro plunked himself down next to James on the ledge. Then he proceeded to chatter for about fifteen minutes. When he finally stopped for breath, he looked up at James with a queer look on his face. He said something that seemed like, "You don't understand a word I'm saying, do you?"

James shrugged his shoulders and said, "You could say anything you wanted to me. You could spit on the grave of my father, and I wouldn't know the difference."

That did it. Kyaro took his response as a request to learn their language and designated himself to be the teacher.

He took James's hand and showed him the ladder to Anasan's roof, pointing to it and naming it. James imitated the sound, over and over, until Kyaro was satisfied. Then the younger boy went back along the ledge and scrambled down to wait for James. James still went slowly, feeling one by one for the toeholds. The wooden ladder was better, though shaky. James came down beside Kyaro, wiped his hands on his legs where his jeans should have been, and looked up at the descent. Kyaro poked him in the ribs and laughed. He said something that James interpreted as meaning, "Come on, chicken!" He went down the next two ladders and into the square without waiting for James.

James followed carefully and turned off the bottom rung into a group of faces. All the women had come to see him; some looked with awe, some with suspicion, scrutinizing every difference about him. One even reached out and drew her finger along his tan line, as though inspecting for dirt. He turned around, shocked, and she pulled back into the group. But there was Kyaro. For a little kid, he sure had a lot of guts. He pointed to each of the women, calling them by name, and having James repeat each name until he said it right. Now that he knew their names, the women were less rude, and Kyaro pulled James through their throng. He had a righteous look on his face that James didn't believe for an instant. But the women shifted to make room and, as the two boys crossed the plaza, turned back to their work.

Kyaro led James into a kiva. All he could see from above was a ladder poking out of a hole. They had to climb through at least five feet of ceiling before coming into the kiva chamber itself. The ladder went over the fire pit, which was smoking but not hot. The room was a perfect circle with six stone pillars in the walls supporting the crossbeams of the roof. A stone bench ran all the way around, breaking only for an air vent.

Kyaro went over to the bench and shoved away some skins that were lying there. It looked as if this room was used a lot, from all the things that were spread around. Along with some more skins, there were a couple of pipes sitting on the bench and a loom set up on the floor with some cloth in the process of being woven. A pit in the floor was covered with lengths of wood. James tapped one with his foot and it thrummed with sound. Kyaro turned around and motioned James to be quiet.

Kyaro picked up a painted wooden shape and handed it to James. It was the head of a bird painted in bright blues and greens. It looked like a parrot or a macaw. It was simple but splendid. "That's really great," said James.

Kyaro took the figure from James and pointed to himself. "This bird is me," he seemed to be saying. James gave him a questioning look. So Kyaro said, "Kyaro," pointing to the bird, then, "Kyaro," pointing to himself.

"I get it," said James. "Your name means Bird, or Parrot, or something like that. That's nice to know."

Kyaro nodded and put the figure back down. Then he pulled a leather bag out of a niche in the wall and motioned for James to sit beside him. From this bag he pulled out several smaller pouches and laid them on the bench. He tipped some yellow dust from one into the palm of his hand. Humming a low tune, he touched his thumb to the dust and smeared a streak across James's forehead. Then Kyaro drew two diagonal lines across his chest. James glanced down to see what it looked like, but Kyaro said, "Oup!" and clicked his tongue violently. So James looked up again, amused by how bossy the boy was.

Kyaro turned dramatically to face the wall and blew the remainder of the yellow dust away. Then he reached for another of the small bags. He had just poured some blue powder into his hand when a foot stepped on the top rung of the ladder. Quickly he brushed the powder off on his leg, leaving a blue streak. Then he stuffed the pouches into the bag and shoved that back in its hole. He was just turning around when the man stepped into the kiva.

The man was younger than Anasan, but still old enough to be Kyaro's father. From the way he was talking to Kyaro, he probably was his father. Kyaro looked so meek and contrite that James almost laughed out loud. But the man gave him a look that said, "You watch it, buddy," so James stopped smiling.

Then the man lit into Kyaro with sharp, quiet words

until the boy's shoulders hunched up in shame. He was sent up the stairs with a swat on his behind, and James followed after, not daring to look at the older man's face.

Up through the roof, James could see Kyaro already ten feet away, dancing with eagerness to get going. James felt awfully conspicuous coming out of the kiva that way, with the yellow stripes on his face and the man still down there, so he just went after Kyaro without looking around. When they'd reached the edge of the terrace, James heard Spring Rain call out his name, and he turned to look. But just as he turned, the man came up out of the kiva, so James scrambled down the hillside after Kyaro.

The two of them picked their way down to the bottom of the mesa. When they were on flat land, James turned to look back up at the village, but all he could see was the rubble-strewn hillside and the retaining wall. He shrugged and went on after Kyaro.

Kyaro skipped ahead and spun around to see if James was keeping up. Usually James didn't mind going barefoot, but he was used to doing it on a smooth green lawn. The only green around here was scruffy juniper and some little cactuses, and their spines tended to fall into the hard-packed sand where James was walking. Kyaro grew impatient when James paused to pull out the spines, and he called out in a whiny, insistent voice. James ignored him. *If he's got to have me along, he's got to put up with my speed,* James thought.

They skirted around the base of the mesa until they came to a place where some rocks had fallen. These formed a jagged stairway up to the cliff wall. There were some figures painted on the wall, and Kyaro scrambled up the rocks to show them to James. James climbed dutifully. But when Kyaro tried to act out what the paintings were saying, James couldn't help but laugh. He didn't get it at all. Something to do with waving arms and jumping up and down and little squiggly things with his fingers.

Then with a grin, Kyaro gave up. He bent down and gathered together a small pile of red dirt from the top of the rock. Squatting, he stuck his hand underneath his loin cloth and directed a stream of urine onto the dirt. James looked the other way, disgusted. When he turned back, Kyaro was stirring the mud with a point of yucca. Then he pounded the yucca between two rocks to open up the strings inside. He wiped these strings in the red mud and stretched up to the wall to make a picture. It was a circle, but pretty sloppy. It was missing a corner; maybe he meant it to be that way, but the edges were all crooked too. Now that he thought of it, all these paintings were pretty uneven. This was probably Kyaro's private painting spot.

James looked up at the smaller boy slapping paint on the wall and smiled until Kyaro turned around and pointed to him. "James," he said. Then he pointed to the wall.

"What?" James asked, pretending not to understand. Kyaro scraped up a small pile of red dirt for James. Then he reached over to James's apron and lifted it up. James whacked his arm away. "Hey!" he shouted. "What do you think you're doing? No way—I'm not going to pee on that."

Kyaro stood back, holding his arm where James had slapped it; he looked shocked and wounded. James turned away and bent over the dirt. He spit as much saliva on the dirt as he could scrape up. It was a compromise, but when he looked again at Kyaro, the boy seemed to be pleased. He handed James his piece of yucca to stir it with, and James produced a thick, dry mud. It didn't spread very well with the yucca brush, so James used his fingers. He smeared a circle, like Kyaro did, but left a smaller circle open in the center. He smiled to himself as he did it. When he was finished, he stepped back and let Kyaro admire his work.

Kyaro was quite articulate in his appreciation of the design. He redrew it with a stick in the sand, explaining all its symbolic meaning to James. James listened, smiling. When Kyaro was finally quiet, James said, "Actually it's just a CD," and he burst out laughing. Kyaro looked at him curiously, which made James laugh all the harder, so Kyaro had to laugh too.

CHAPTER XX

I need help," cried Tsira, who was only three summers old. She had more clay on her fingers than on the pot. She was trying to squeeze out a bowl, so Spring Rain showed her how to roll clay between the palms of her hands to make a snake. She still couldn't do it, but it made less of a mess. Sakwa, who was already five, was doing fine. She had rolls and coils up around a base now. She smiled at Spring Rain and kept on working. The baby was sucking on the clay, so Spring Rain took it away and gave him a small turkey bone instead. She had a bag of small playthings that she brought with her when she took care of the children.

"Who is the stranger?" asked Sakwa.

"What was that?" said Spring Rain.

"Who is the strange man?"

"His name is James," replied Spring Rain.

"Nobody has a name like that," said the little girl. "What does it mean?"

"It just means James."

"That's silly," said Sakwa. "How come he can't talk?"

"He can talk," Spring Rain answered, "just not like us."

"Does he talk to Anasan?"

"Yes," said Spring Rain, "and Anasan talks to him; but they don't understand each other."

"Why does he talk if nobody understands him?" asked Sakwa.

"His people understand him."

"Who are they?"

"I don't know," said Spring Rain.

"Is he going to be your man, or is Kyaro?" Sakwa asked.

Spring Rain looked at the little girl, shocked. "Who told you that?" she asked.

"I just heard."

It was awful to hear gossip repeated by the children. People don't think little ones have ears. Sakwa was sitting there patiently waiting for an answer. It was hard to get mad at a five-year-old for asking a question, even if it was none of her business. "I don't know," she said, finally. "Kyaro is too young, and James is, well, I don't know about James."

Sakwa nodded seriously and turned back to her clay pot. She was satisfied, but Spring Rain was not. All Anasan wanted her to do was get a child, but it didn't just happen like that. The man at least had to be interested in her, and Kyaro definitely was not ready. James was interested, but what kind of man was he? The village was not impressed. If he was going to father their leader, he should at least be a great hunter, or be able to grow wonderful corn, or read the signs in the sky. He hasn't asked to go hunting, he just wanders after her or Kyaro and doesn't do anything much. The village wasn't impressed, and neither was Spring Rain.

"Sakwa," she said suddenly, "go down to the edge of the plaza and see if you can spot Kyaro and James."

Sakwa jumped up obligingly and went to see. She shook her head from where she stood at the retaining wall. Spring Rain pounded her fist into her clay.

"What's the matter?" asked Sakwa when she got back.

"They should be back by now. They've been gone a long time."

"Not so long," said Sakwa. She worked on her bowl for a minute. The other children were throwing clay pieces at each other, mostly hitting the ground between them. "Why are you angry?" Sakwa asked.

Spring Rain looked at the little girl and shook her head. "You wouldn't understand," she said. What right did those two have to just go off and not tell her when they were coming back, or where they were going? First Kyaro takes him in the kiva, even though it is forbidden to bring a stranger there. He thinks he can get away with anything because he is a boy. Then he takes James off into the desert. What if something happens to James? She pushed the thoughts out of her mind and concentrated very hard on smoothing the base of the bowl.

CHAPTER XXI

James and Kyaro walked away from the cliff chuckling and wiping their eyes. Back in the village, everyone seemed busy except Spring Rain, who sat on a rooftop with the children. She was gazing off into space, paying no attention to what the kids were doing. When James and Kyaro climbed up over the retaining wall, her head snapped around to look at them.

"Spring Rain," called Kyaro. She turned away. He looked at James and shrugged his shoulders. They went up to the house where she was.

"Hey, Spring Rain," James said. They were near enough now that she could hear his voice even though he spoke softly. She turned around with a great show of reluctance. James smiled up at her stony face. He had no idea what was bothering her. Her eyes were bright black as she spoke with quiet, furious words at Kyaro. The boy pretended to be contrite. He looked down at his toes and traced little patterns in the sand. But he held his hands behind his back, wiggling his fingers to mock her gestures. He annoyed James.

When she paused, Kyaro said something that seemed to mean, "Have you finished? May I go now?" And he scooted away before she answered.

Spring Rain turned to James, and he shrugged his shoulders. "What can I say? He's just a kid," he said.

But that wasn't enough for her. James had been with Kyaro, so he too was at fault, whatever it was they had done. Spring Rain gave James a cold look, turned her back, and ignored him.

All of a sudden, James felt impotent against this anger. His stomach clenched, and he felt lost. Where would he be without Spring Rain? How would he get home again? And then the thought washed over him that he might not ever get back. He sat down on the ground with his face in his hands. All he wanted was his own time. All he wanted was to go home.

He felt her kneel down beside him, but he didn't look up. She took his chin in her hands and pulled his face up to look at hers. He didn't hide the fear from his eyes. And she smiled.

The smile worked. It was like a gulp of coffee when you're dead cold. James closed his eyes, brushed his hand across them, and brought his smile back up from his stomach. He looked at Spring Rain, who still had her hands on his chin. She was the loveliest girl he'd ever seen.

"Spring Rain," called a woman from over by the houses. Spring Rain started, and got up quickly. When she came back, she carried a clay pot on her head. She called the children together. James didn't wait to be invited. He picked up the little baby boy, took the hand of a slightly older girl, and went after Spring Rain. She looked surprised that James was holding the baby, but she smiled warmly and skipped down the mesa path.

They went around the foot of the mesa until they came to a place where a few low bushes were growing against the stone. Spring Rain bent back the branches. There was a pot nestled in the sand patiently catching water that dripped from a crack in the cliff. Spring Rain replaced the full pot with the empty one she'd brought along. The children played in the soft sand, keeping to the shade of the cliff.

It was hot. James sat down and looked up at the sky, burned pale by the sun. The little boy he'd carried crawled up on his leg. James bounced him a bit; then they played peek-a-boo. The baby was delighted. When he giggled, his smile showed two top teeth, and he put his arms across his face to hide. James loved it. He didn't get much chance to play with babies at home. The other two children stopped their games to watch. James picked up the baby and did "this little piggy" with his toes. The others stretched out their legs and shyly wiggled their toes, so James had to do "this little piggy" on all of them.

By the time he was finished, Spring Rain was more than ready to go back. The children lined up at the drip in the rock and bent over for a lick of water. James followed their example, hoping to get a fresh cool mouthful, but he was only able to wet his tongue. It tasted like warm mud. James stopped himself from thinking of his water bottle at the top of the cliff.

The walk back was hotter, and the drip of water was

only a tease to his thirsty throat. The little boy, who was such fun to play with in the shade, was a sleepy hot lump in the sun. The other two children pulled on James's spare arm while Spring Rain walked on ahead. She balanced the water jug firmly on the top of her head.

When James had to shake the children loose so he could pull a thorn out of his foot, Spring Rain noticed without turning around, and waited for him. *She may be moody,* he thought, *but she's a whole lot nicer than Kyaro.*

Back in the village, all the little kids found a shady spot where they could curl up. When James set down his bundle, the baby sleepily stuck his toes out for one more tug. So James whispered "piggy" to him, and he dozed off. The whole village was quiet. *Siesta time,* thought James. He went with Spring Rain up to Anasan's house. The old man was sleeping too. They passed by the doorway and climbed on up to the crack in the rocks.

They sat down, facing each other, in the cool shade of the cave. This was nice. James watched Spring Rain's sweet face for a moment, then closed his eyes. As he was dozing off, he was aware of her hand on his foot, rubbing gently. He slept, completely relaxed.

His dream brought him home. But not home as he'd left it. The house was a ruin, walls broken down, and the roof just rubble on the floor. It was totally silent. Even his slight whimpering echoed in the empty, ruined rooms. His whimper increased to a cry, then he was weeping and shouting, "Grandad, what about the coffee!?"

142

Spring Rain woke him up and brushed his tears off his cheeks. She pressed the palm of her hand in his center, just below his ribs, and rubbed where the soreness from the dream lingered.

"What's going on, Spring Rain? Will I ever get home again? My God, how will I ever get home?" The hopelessness of his situation overwhelmed him for the second time that day, and this time he was too exhausted to fight it off. He bent over his bare, dusty knees and sobbed.

Spring Rain wrapped her arms around him and rocked back and forth. She started humming in that funny voice of hers, then singing. James knew the songs. He knew them from both times, before and now.

After a while, he sat up and asked her to sing one over and over so he could learn it. Slowly, making all the wrong sounds at first, he copied her tune. Then he wanted to know what it meant. So Spring Rain untied a sharp stone from her apron belt and scraped a picture on the sandstone wall.

She drew a straight line with a hole in the middle. Underneath the hole she scratched a stick man. Then above the line she drew a round figure with eight legs— maybe a spider, he thought. She pointed to the spider and showed how he walked up over the line, and then she showed how the man figure followed the spider up. She sang the lines to the song slowly as her fingers told the story.

Pretty slim story, thought James. *It probably lost something in the translation.* "Hey, Spring Rain," he said, "have you heard this: 'Row, row, row your boat, gently down the stream. . . .' " He picked up her stone and scraped a small rowboat over some ripples to indicate water. Spring Rain looked mystified. So James drew a man inside the boat pulling on two oars. "See, he's rowing: 'Row, row, row your boat.' "

"Ro ro ro yo bo," imitated Spring Rain.

James burst out laughing. "Row your boat!" he chuckled.

"Ro yo bo," repeated Spring Rain, starting to smile. "Ro ro ro yo bo bo bo." The sounds ran off into giggles. She pointed up to the wavy lines. "Bo bo bo?" she asked.

"No!" shouted James hysterically. He pointed shakily to the rowboat.

"No," she said, pointing to the boat.

"No, boat!"

Her face was flaming with laughter. "Noboat" she said.

James could only shake his head. "Rowboat," he gasped. "On the water—those waves are water, don't you know?"

Spring Rain was still laughing. The thought struck him that she had never seen that much water in her whole life. The only water she knew was the rare rainfall and the few drips from the cliff spring.

She noticed his look and ran her fingers on his cheek. What is it? they seemed to say.

"It's just the sound of a lot of water, Spring Rain," James answered. "I just realized you're never going to hear that wild sound of rushing water. Unless the San Juan fills up again. Now that's a river, heavy, deep, and fast. I rafted down it once, and it was amazing."

Spring Rain listened tight to each word; and when he stopped talking, she sat back against the cool wall and moved her lips silently, as if still hearing and trying to make the sounds he made.

CHAPTER XXII

Teaching James to talk was a slow process. He didn't know any words at all, not even how to say, "What is this?" So she had to start with pictures, the way she did for her name, and with pointing. "Sky," she would say, and point to the sky; "yellow corn," and she held a handful of corn. It was slow, and he sounded silly, like Tsira who was just starting to talk. Actually, he learned some words while he was playing with the little girl. Tsira learned some of his words as well, like that "piki" chant he did on her feet.

Kyaro was a help too, although she couldn't trust him to teach James the right words for things. It would be just like him to say, with his eyes wide open in innocence, that the word for "bread" is "turkey dirt."

Spring Rain was sitting on the retaining wall thinking about going up to bed when Kyaro came over to her. She had already taken James up to Anasan's hut, but Kyaro had been up there waiting for James. So Spring Rain just turned and went back down without even saying, "Sleep in peace." She didn't want to share James.

So she wasn't very welcoming when Kyaro walked up to her and stared at her feet.

"Nice toes," he said.

She covered them with her hands, and said, "What do you want?"

"What do you think of James?" he asked.

"What do you mean, what do I think?"

"I mean, do you like him or not?" said Kyaro.

"What difference does it make to you?" said Spring Rain. "Why don't you take care of your own problems."

"I don't care one way or the other," said Kyaro. "He just asked me to ask you."

"He did what?"

"He said, 'Kyaro, does Spring Rain like me? Why does she act nice one time and ignore me the next? Does she think I am not a real man?'" Kyaro spoke the false message as if he were James, talking in an accent and making mistakes.

Spring Rain was disgusted. "Look, green feathers, if you want to ask me questions, go ahead and ask. But don't shame our visitor and friend by putting words into his mouth."

"All right, so he didn't say that. But he wants to know anyway. I've been watching how you act toward him, and anyone would be confused. But if you want to hear the question from me, I'll ask you. How do you feel about James? Do you think he is just bad at doing everything he ought to be able to do, but nice anyway; or do you think he is a flea altogether, and you'd rather he left you alone?"

Spring Rain spoke slowly. "I don't think that he is so incapable," she said. "He is wonderful with the children."

"I said," said Kyaro, "in all the things he ought to be able to do, things a man should be able to do."

Spring Rain nodded. "That's what the villagers think, isn't it?"

"It is the truth," said Kyaro. "He can't run. He can't hit a tree with an arrow, much less a moving rabbit. He doesn't know how to weave. He even had to be shown how to make an earth mound for the sprouting corn. He's never smoked a pipe, and he doesn't know a single dance; but he is good at all the things he does with you. Doesn't that make you wonder?"

"You are awful," said Spring Rain. "He's only been here half a moon. You have to give him a chance to learn."

"What kind of man is he that he has to learn these basic things?" asked Kyaro in a quiet voice. "What kind of tribe could he come from where he didn't learn them as a child?"

"Maybe he has a different kind of gift," suggested Spring Rain.

Kyaro shook his head and stood up. "You never told me how you felt about him," he said, turning to go.

"Yes, I did," said Spring Rain, "you just weren't listening."

* * *

A few days later, James went along when Spring Rain and the children were cutting yucca out in the desert. Spring Rain carried the baby on a sling at her waist, and James carried little Tsira across the desert so she wouldn't get tired. Sakwa was old enough to walk on her own.

Spring Rain and James each had a sharp stone knife that they used to hack off the yucca spikes, and the children would gather them in a basket. Tsira kept rubbing the spikes the wrong way and cutting her fingers. It was a slow process.

Spring Rain was trying to get James to talk, but he always mixed up the words. It was frustrating, and she was hot. She wanted to give up. Kyaro was right, this man was incapable of everything except the simple things that women do. If he didn't start talking like a man, and acting like a man, how could she explain to the villagers how much she wanted him? He burned a slow fire in her center: just being near him made her glow. She didn't want to wait for Kyaro to become a man. Anasan didn't want her to wait.

She put her knife down for a moment and helped the children pick up the rest of the pieces. Sakwa, the oldest, started singing a song, a simple one that even Tsira could sing. James joined in. He listened carefully, and eventually got the words right. It was so wonderful that they sang it all the way back to the village. But when they got there and the children were set to sleep, James asked, "What is?" and he sang the song again. He had all the words right, but he didn't know what any of them meant.

Hey, hey, day is one
Corn is planted in the sun.
Hey, hey, sun is yellow,
Hey, hey, rain is blue.

Hey, hey, day is two
Corn is yellow, corn is blue.
Hey, hey, sun is yellow,
Hey, hey, rain is blue.

Hey, hey, day is three
Sun and rain grow corn so green.
Hey, hey, sun is yellow,
Hey, hey, rain is blue.

" 'Hey, hey,' " said James, struggling with the Anasazi words. "What is?"

"Nothing," said Spring Rain, shaking her head. "Just a sound. But the next word, 'day' that is one sun and one moon full." She drew the picture of a sun and a moon, and drew a circle around them. "Day," she said.

"Day," said James.

She smiled at him. "Sun," she said, pointing to the picture of the sun.

"Sun," said James, "day sun."

"Yes," said Spring Rain. "Day sun, night moon." She pointed to the picture of the moon and closed her eyes. Then she pointed to the sun, and said "sun," to the moon and said "moon." "Day," she said with her eyes open, "and night" her eyes were closed.

"Sun moon day night," said James. "Sun day, moon night."

Spring Rain clapped her hands out loud. Maybe they were getting somewhere. They sang the song over and over while they pounded the yucca into fibers and the children slept through the heat.

CHAPTER XXIII

Life in this strange situation was settling into a routine. James spent his days with Spring Rain or with Kyaro. They were the only two people who had enough patience to try and communicate with him. He was trying his best to learn their language, but it was incredibly hard. None of the words made sense to him; he felt like he'd been dropped down in Outer Mongolia, except he hadn't traveled anywhere really. He kept mixing up the sounds and thinking one word was another.

Spring Rain got very frustrated with him when he kept twisting words. She would make him repeat something over and over until he got it perfect. Then in a couple of hours, she would ask him what it was. Sometimes he'd remember, but other times he'd stumble, and she would lay into him with a stream of "Why can't you ever get it right? It is so easy!" He was, at least, starting to understand the basic gist of what people were saying. The melody of the language was beginning to make sense. If he actually knew one word out of twenty in a conversation, he was lucky; but by being attuned to what was going on, and the tone and shape of what was being said, he could figure out a little. It was much better than being in a vacuum the way he was for the first few weeks.

Kyaro was more forgiving. He seemed to enjoy the mistakes, making a great joke out of them before telling James the right way. Because of this, James was more relaxed around Kyaro and seemed to be able to say more to him.

It felt like Kyaro had taken James on as a special project. He was doing his best to train him in all things Anasazi—language, hunting, trapping, taking care of the crops; he even taught James how to spin cotton and showed him the loom. It was as if he were trying to make James acceptable to the village. They certainly had a lot of negative feelings about him. He felt it most at mealtimes when they begrudged him the food he ate—and he barely even ate anything.

Today they were out in the desert, and Kyaro was teaching him to use the bow. James had taken archery in 4-H, but those fiberglass bows were flimsy compared to this. Kyaro used a stiff branch roughly tapered at both ends, strung with a thin rawhide strip. The arrow fitted neatly on the string, and when Kyaro shot it, it flew straight and far.

When James tried it, though, the arrow kept slipping off the string even before he pulled it back. When he figured out how to hold it properly between his fingers, the string gave a little *thwang* and the arrow curved out and down, ten miserable feet away. Kyaro stood on the side and gave out pointers. At least James was getting some language out of this. Kyaro spent about half the time showing James how to do something and the other half teaching him the words.

After a couple of hours, Kyaro decided he was ready for target practice. Kyaro pointed out a paper wasp's nest high in a scrawny cedar. It was a big target—Kyaro would knock it down, no problem, from fifty feet away. But for James it was not only difficult, it was plain embarrassing. If he missed the nest and hit the tree, the arrow would be too high to reach. James didn't know the policy for lost arrows, but if it had to be retrieved, it looked like scratchy climbing on skinny branches. If it stayed there, it would be a sure sign for everyone to see what a lousy shot he was.

Kyaro said, "Go on, shoot it!"

James kept inching forward, until he finally stood just ten feet from the tree. Exasperated, Kyaro said, "If you can't make it from here, forget it!" or something to that effect. So James fitted the arrow to the string. He looked up the length of the arrow at the nest. "Are you sure it's empty?" he asked. Then he held his breath, shut his eyes, and let fly.

He heard a ripping sound and something soft dropped to the ground. It was the nest, split open. But where was the other half? Still shaking from the impact, the arrow stuck in the split wasp's nest, hanging twelve feet high, impossible to reach.

James turned around. Kyaro was shaking his head, smiling a little, but not laughing like James expected.

Kyaro said, "Let's go," and they turned their backs on the arrow and walked to the village.

He spent the afternoon alone. Kyaro had gone down into the kiva where James wasn't welcome, and Spring Rain was busy with the women while the children slept. So James took off down the desert path. He decided he would walk around the entire mesa to see if he could get a sense of where he was in relation to the rest of the world.

The growing fields were just beyond the water spring. Four people were there, weeding the young plants so they would grow strong. They didn't even look up as James walked past. He wondered if he would ever stop being an extra in the community. For the most part, he was ignored, which was better that being hated outright, he guessed.

But if he had to be here for a long time, he would need to be thought of as useful. It was a good thing that Kyaro was training him. There were all sorts of things that he could do that made no sense at all to these people: fix a car, read and write, use a computer, even whip up a milk shake. What a waste. *It is a waste of my life to spend it here,* he thought angrily. *How will I ever get home? It's not as if I came here in a machine, and all I had to do was push the return button. I wish it were that simple.*

Walking barefoot on the sand, James's footsteps were quieter, and he was more alert than he'd ever been before. He heard the distinctive rustle of a rattlesnake and circled around the sound. Halfway up the red cliff, a hawk wheeled, a silhouette of wings on the crisp blue sky. The desert was still, hot, and beautiful. If James were only when he belonged, this would be perfect, this peace.

He tried to think about Grandad, but it hurt him in the stomach, so he thought about his mother instead. With her, there was always a layer of anger, so he could distance the longing. What would she think of this experience? What would she say when he didn't come back? Would she be relieved, no more child to deal with? Then she'd only have an aging father between her and total independence.

It occurred to James that it must have hurt her a whole lot when his father left. Even though he had never even seen a picture of his father, James was sure that he must look a lot more like him than his mom. Maybe that was why she stayed away. Maybe he reminded her of what a failure she was. If the only thing you feel around someone is pain, then it sure must be hard to spend time with him. His mom had never spent enough time with James for her to have any good times at all. He'd never been given the chance to show her how much fun he could be. Hell, Grandad didn't love him for nothing. But his mother didn't even know who he was.

He walked and walked, around the mesa, over the land that was so dry it cracked, and tears dropped from his eyes and evaporated on his cheeks. He didn't even bother to wipe the tracks in the dust.

He was tired and all dried up when he got back around to the village. He saw Spring Rain up on Anasan's ledge, so he climbed up to be with her. They went up together to the cave in the rock.

Spring Rain was quiet. He couldn't tell if she was angry or just depressed. Whenever he was gone for any length of time with Kyaro, it took a while for her to warm up to him again. But he felt it was important to spend time away from her.

She just sat against the wall, drawn into herself. James sat beside her fidgeting. It was hot, and he got tired of waiting. Finally he stood up to go find Kyaro. Better getting into trouble with him than sweating it out with Spring Rain. But she put up her hand to restrain him. He looked down, and she had a sad, anxious look on her face. James almost blew up with frustration. "Well, what do you want, Spring Rain?" he asked. He was furious that she couldn't understand him, that, for all the time they had shared together, they couldn't share their ideas and thoughts. "First you sit there, paying no attention to anyone but yourself, then you complain when I want to leave." He was speaking in English. He tried again, forcing his mind to come up with some Anasazi word to fit the situation. He had none. Finally he just said, "What?"

She started talking, fast and full of emotion. The words washed over him like the heat, and he ignored them. This was as bad as before, only now he had to pretend he was interested and listening. So he sat there, waiting for her to stop, and tried not to think about his grandfather, his room, a root beer float. . . .

When the words stopped, he hardly noticed. He was looking out the crack at a cloud blowing across the sky. He didn't know when she started to cry, but when he was aware of it, somehow the silent tears made more noise than all her words. He put his arms around her, and her head fell into his shoulder. He rubbed the small of her back.

As she relaxed, the sobbing began for real. Deep, silent heaves against which James had no protection. He just held her, not moving, and felt her tears run down his skin, already salty with sweat. When it was all over, she curled in his lap, and he leaned up against the wall.

CHAPTER XXIV

Spring Rain didn't sleep very well that night. When she had brought James up here in the afternoon, she brought him to her bed. She hadn't thought of it like that then. It was only when she woke up with her head in his lap and looked at him still sleeping. It was as if they were already in their own hut together. Then he woke up, he looked right into her eyes, and he picked her up around the shoulders and pressed his lips into hers. His tongue was alive in her mouth, and she was spinning.

Lying down now on the cool rock, with the blanket pulled up around her shoulders, she felt his touch over and over in her mind. She tried not to remember how suddenly he had turned away. They were so still, holding each other and breathing at the same time. All at once, he mumbled something, and went to the edge of the rock. It was almost dark, and the fires set the great cave aglow. She went up behind him and put her hands on the top of his back and rubbed deep softness into his skin. For a moment, he relaxed, then he turned around and said, "Go—"

So she dropped her hands to her sides and followed his slow, careful steps across the cliffside to Anasan's roof.

At the door opening, James reached up his hand and let it sit on her cheek an instant. She felt as if a butterfly had settled there, and dared not move. Then he went inside, greeted warmly by Anasan: "Good end-of-day, my stranger son. Have you pleased the girl today?"

If only James understood him, Spring Rain thought, and told him just how pleased I am. She turned, singing inside, to go up again to her room.

Before she was halfway up the ladder, though, she heard Kyaro calling her from below. "Spring Rain! Heyah, Spring Rain!" He waved his arms wildly for her to come down. So she did, reluctantly.

He wanted to talk about James. Since he was on Spring Rain's mind too, she agreed. They went over to a deserted firepit and sat down close to the dying embers.

"You know what happened today?" Kyaro asked.

Spring Rain waited for him to tell.

"James was shooting the bow, and on his first try, he hit a wasp's nest way in the top of a tree."

"His first try?" Spring Rain was skeptical.

"Well, he practiced shooting for a while, but it was his first try at hitting something real," said Kyaro.

"So, that's good," said Spring Rain.

"But that's not all," said Kyaro excitedly. "Only half the nest fell to the ground. He split it directly in half and the arrow stayed, shaking in the piece on the tree."

"Is the arrow still there?"

Kyaro nodded. "Don't you see? It's amazing. I don't even mind losing an arrow. It must be a sign. Something was guiding his arrow."

"I think it was an accident," said Spring Rain.

"Look, Spring Rain," said Kyaro. "What I said about James being not much of a man—well, I'm telling you this to take it back." Spring Rain arched her eyebrows at him. "All he has to do is learn," explained Kyaro. "And I'm teaching him."

Spring Rain started to smile, but thought better of it. "Kyaro," she said, "it's time I told you something. Your mother, and half the village, I guess, want you to be my man."

"Oh, that," replied Kyaro. "I know. But I'm not old enough to be anyone's man. I'm not ready for that, Spring Rain. James is, though."

"I know," said Spring Rain.

Kyaro looked at her and grinned. "The way I figure it is this," he began.

"Have you got everything figured out?" Spring Rain asked.

"Just listen," said Kyaro. "Now, James isn't going to be here forever." Spring Rain drew in her breath, but Kyaro kept on. "He came all of a sudden, and he'll go all of a sudden, like your father. People who stay here were born here. You know. But he is here right now, and you two have a bond between you. You found him, after all." He stopped talking for a moment, thinking.

"Hey, Spring Rain, were you singing when he came? Did you sing him here? Is he the one who was listening?"

"I think so," Spring Rain answered quietly.

Kyaro thought for a minute, then he pounded his fist into his hand. "I'm sure that's it. You should be together now, and I'll have you later, in a few years, if that's how it happens."

"And what if he wants to stay? What if he can't go?"

"Then I'll have Sakwa, or someone. But I'd rather have you."

"Why are you so mature all of a sudden?" asked Spring Rain.

"I've been working on this for a long time," said Kyaro. "Besides, my mother has been bothering me. There she is, over there." He pointed to his doorway where Raina stood watching them. "My mother is pleased that we are talking." He grinned and went on, "I've been trying to teach James. You know, things he has to do to survive; hunt and trap and find plants to eat. He didn't know any of it before, but he's learning."

Spring Rain nodded. Kyaro looked at her for a minute, then asked, "Remember the story of how your father won your mother?"

"Of course."

"Well, my mother wants me to do the same thing. James is the stranger and I am the only challenger. You see, I could propose a contest between us. If he just stepped in and took you by flattery, the village wouldn't approve."

"But he could never win a contest," said Spring Rain.

"It would just be me and him," Kyaro explained. "Nobody would be there to see what happened."

"You mean you would kill something and say it was

his?" asked Spring Rain. "That wouldn't be right."

"No, I wouldn't have to do that," said Kyaro. "I just don't have to make my kill very important. Then I can help James find the right spot and the right trap, but let him do his killing alone. What do you think? I can make the challenge tomorrow."

"It sounds like a good idea," said Spring Rain. "Are you sure he's ready?"

"I'll make sure he's ready."

CHAPTER XXV

The next morning, Spring Rain came down from the crevice where she was sleeping and woke James up with a light touch. He smiled up at her, and they went out to stand on the ledge where Anasan was already. It was nice being there, just the three of them, watching the night sky change into day colors. They were looking out across the desert beyond the village, scanning for rain clouds, as Anasan did every morning. It was wonderful, the warmth and the stillness. The red desert stretched out flat until away in the distance it layered itself up into another mesa. The sky was cloudless, a pale hazy blue. There would be no rain today.

Someone in the village was shouting. James didn't pay any attention until Spring Rain nudged him. Kyaro was down there calling up to him. He carried a bundle under his arm, and he was waving his hand up to James and pointing to his bundle, explaining loudly. James heard the word "go" but he had no idea what it was referring to. Spring Rain smiled broadly; of course she understood. She disappeared into Anasan's hut and came out a minute later and gave James a bundle of stuff tied in his blanket. She gestured to Kyaro and then gave James a shove.

"Now, wait a minute!" James said. "What is going on?" He set down the blanket and faced Spring Rain with his hands on his hips.

So she called down to Kyaro, and he climbed up to the second-story rooftop. They took turns trying to explain to James what was happening, but the concept was too complicated. He couldn't get a clue.

Spring Rain squatted down and drew pictures on the dirt, explaining with gestures and simple words that James was to go with Kyaro on a trip. They would take four days, and they would do some hunting. *What about asking me if I wanted to go?* thought James. But he picked up his bundle and set off after Kyaro.

They made good time, striding across the desert sand. After a while James broke the silence. "What are we hunting for?" he asked. He was able to translate the most important words so that Kyaro understood the question. But the answer wasn't very satisfactory.

"Food," said the boy.

At noon they stopped for water. In each of their packs was a clay jug. They dipped two fingers in and ran their tongues along the drip. They sat in the shade of a piñon tree, which spread its thin, evergreen branches out in the hot air. Its dusty dark color looked artificial in the middle of this dry, red sand. The drip of water hadn't done a thing to quench James's thirst. He curled his toes around a small rock and it crumbled into dust.

Kyaro spoke to James, pointing across the desert, toward a distant mesa. That was where they were heading. Back in the sun, they walked for a minute, then Kyaro started to jog-trot. They had often run around the village like this; it seemed more comfortable for Kyaro than walking. James ran around the track at home sometimes, and he was in decent shape. But he questioned how far he could go with little water or food in this hot sun.

They kept going, and the only thing that changed was the sun in the sky and the mesa. They kept it at a distance, to their left. Slowly they moved around it. James was hungry and dry. His legs felt as if they were no longer a part of his body. But Kyaro kept going with no sign of letting up, so James just let his legs keep slapping the dirt.

His mind drifted away from the view of cactus and red sand. He crawled home, into his safe bedroom with the covers pulled up to his neck, and he was picturing his walls, one by one. Then, in his imagination, Grandad knocked on the door and came in.

"Oh!" James said aloud, and the jolt of being back in the desert, without his room, without Grandad, was too much.

He pulled up short, panting and holding his side. "Kyaro!" he called. "Wait up! I have to rest! *Stop,*" he called out in Anasazi. Kyaro came back and waited for James.

"What the hell am I doing here," James asked, "way off in the middle of nowhere?"

Kyaro must have understood the dismal tone of voice, if not the words, because he came up to James and poked his shoulders. "Hey uh nunna," said the boy in a bouncy, chanting voice. "Hey uh nunna, hey uh nunna hey." James listened, and when he had learned the tune, Kyaro taught him a pattern of snaps, slaps, and claps that went along with it.

click-click slap-slap; click-click slap-slap
click-click slap-slap; clap

They started out again, keeping time with each other through the song. After a while, Kyaro threw in variations to the rhythm section. James picked them up and sent back others, slightly changed:

click slap clap-clap; click slap clap-clap
click clap slap-slap-slap.

They laughed when their hands fumbled, and after a while, the sun was low. Kyaro stopped, and motioning for James to be quiet, let down his bag and loosened the ties. He pulled out a bow, a small one, less than a yard long, and slipped on its string.

They squatted down and went forward twenty feet. There was a small dip in the land there where some rocks were piled. On the other side of the rocks, James saw a dry stream bed with only slightly moist sand in the center. Kyaro looked at footprints, keeping himself well hidden behind the rocks.

They waited a long time before a rabbit hopped up to the hole. *Let him drink first,* thought James, easy, easy.

Kyaro shot the arrow cleanly into the rabbit's side.

He tied it up by its hind legs onto his pack, and they went on.

When Kyaro finally stopped, James was past being exhausted. The thought of food was almost repulsive. He wet his mouth with the water and lay back in the sand.

Kyaro took his sharp stone knife from his bundle and carefully slit the rabbit skin open. He made a small incision, then worked the knife back and forth. As the skin opened up, he peeled it back like a banana, cutting the connecting tissue. James watched absently.

When the whole skin was off, Kyaro left the meat lying on a flat rock while he rubbed the skin with sand. He had a packet of fine white sand that he rubbed on it next. He licked his fingers when he was done, and offered a taste to James. It was salt, but gritty and dirty. It would cure the skin, James guessed. Kyaro set small stones around the edge to hold it flat.

Then he actually rubbed sticks together to make a fire. Mostly, he worked in silence, but when the fire was flickering, he started talking to James, not saying much, just going on and on.

They roasted the rabbit and ate a piece, then snacked on some seeds. James didn't mind curling up in the soft sand. The untied pack became his blanket, and the earth felt warm under his shoulders.

Something disturbed them in the middle of the night. Kyaro was already crouched over the fire, blowing on the embers, trying to work up a flame. Then James heard it again—the long, low howl of a coyote. A second one answered from the other side. James shivered.

He sat up, still wrapped in his blanket, to help Kyaro with the fire. With a look, Kyaro warned him to keep quiet. James held up two fingers, asking if there were only two coyotes out there. Kyaro shook his head. Here we are in the center, he said with his fingers, and around us are five, maybe more. We have to have more fire.

Now James was scared. Even though coyotes are wild, they're not too threatening one at a time. But in a pack, if they're hungry, it's a different story. As silently as possible, he gathered sticks and brush. He knew if it came to fighting them off, they'd need a heavy stick, lit like a torch. Did he dare go a little farther away from the campsite to find some? He heard a howl, and then a chorus. Yes, the animals were ringed around them, but still a ways off. James touched Kyaro on the shoulder, as if to collect some courage, and then walked away from the dim light.

It seemed that every step James took farther from the fire, the coyotes circled in tighter. He bent over double, searching for wood, as quietly as possible. Finally he found a large, split branch. James ran with it back to the camp and gave half to Kyaro.

The fire was blazing. Luckily the branch had some pitch on it. They roasted their torches in the flames, waiting tensely for the wood to glow.

Kyaro looked at James, his face serious. He picked up his brand and turned his back to the fire. James did the same on the other side.

And just in time. Five coyotes circled curiously

around the fire, their eyes glowing red in its light. James could feel their hot breath, could see their fur move as they paced around and around. One by one, all the coyotes sat down in a ring around the fire. They lifted their muzzles up to the sky and howled, piercing the air. The hairs lifted on James's skin, and the flame wavered. The sound was sinister and close and wild. James forced back a scream. The coyotes lowered their heads and leaned toward the fire, sniffing. As if they objected to the smell, they turned and left in single file.

For a long time, James and Kyaro held their positions, not daring to move. But sleep ached over them. They stuck their branches in the fire, and curled up as close to the flames as they could without burning themselves.

CHAPTER XXVI

The village was quiet without James and Kyaro. Spring Rain went about doing the things that had to be done without much enthusiasm. Her future, and the future of the village, was in Kyaro's hands. What a frightening thought. If he didn't do it right, James would have to go.

If James really had to go, if the villagers refused to share their food with him and ran him out, what would he do? Spring Rain was fairly certain that she was responsible for bringing James here from wherever he came. It could be that he would go back if she sang the song again, the one that she was singing when it started to rain. She had been very careful not to sing even the smallest part of that particular song. She tried not to even think of the melody for fear that it would take James away.

So if the village really became angry, if James came back from this hunt with empty hands and she defied the village by going with him anyway, what then? She knew with all certainty that James was the right man for her son. But there was no explaining this. She knew because of the song, and the villagers did not share this song.

The children were playing a quiet game, and Spring Rain sat by the wall so they wouldn't fall off. She was working on a pair of yucca sandals that would fit James when the nights grew cold. She didn't notice when Sorsi Raina and the baby's mother, Talawi, came over to talk to her.

"Spring Rain!" Raina snapped her fingers in front of the girl's eyes.

She looked up with a jerk. What did they want? They usually didn't bother her when she was with the children. They enjoyed being away by themselves. "What is it?" she asked. Her voice said, "Leave me alone," if her words didn't.

"We want to talk to you about the boys," said Talawi.

"One of them is a man," said Spring Rain.

Kyaro's mother bristled at this statement, but it was Talawi who spoke. "You feel a lot for the stranger, don't you?" she asked.

"He is different from anyone in the village," Spring Rain answered carefully.

"Everyone in the village can care for themselves. He needs you like one of the babies," said Raina.

Talawi interrupted before Spring Rain could retort. "You know," she said gently, "feelings aren't everything." The two women looked pointedly at the sandles in Spring Rain's hands that were so long they could fit only James, but they made no comment.

"We came to talk to you," said Rain, "because we already have men, and thought we should tell you something about what it means to have one."

Spring Rain sighed and leaned back on her hands. They were trying so hard to seem friendly, but there was nothing she hated more than to be told what to do. She put on a smile. "So tell me," she said, "I am listening."

Both Raina and Talawi relaxed and sat on the ground next to her. "Well," said one, and "It's like," said the other, both at the same time. They looked at each other and giggled. Spring Rain held her smile steady.

Talawi started to tell Spring Rain about men. Spring Rain listened patiently for a while, then her mind wandered. Finally she asked, "Where are you going with all your windy words?"

Raina said, "Well, if you want to be rude, we'll just say it. We all know who should win this contest. We all know who is more able. The one who wins will be yours, and you have the right to say, just with a word, that the boy who truly will be a man and not a suckling baby is the one you will have."

Spring Rain had had enough. If they had come over here to try and change her mind about Kyaro and James, they were wrong. But she would have the last word. Straight out, she said: "If you two are worried that I'll take James to be my man and not Kyaro, you can stop worrying. Whoever brings back the best kill will be my man. And if something happens to him, then I will take the other. But no matter who wins, Kyaro will not be my man until he *is* a man."

They had no answer for that. Spring Rain stood up and gathered the children. The baby was clinging to his

173

mother, but Talawi pushed him off her lap, and Sakwa picked him up. They left the two women and went for a walk.

"What did they want, Spring Rain?" asked Sakwa as they walked around the edge of the squash field. Spring Rain was carrying the baby now, and Sakwa held Tsira's hand.

"They were just bothering me," said Spring Rain.

"About Kyaro and the man?"

Spring Rain nodded.

"They want you to have Kyaro, not the stranger, right?" asked Sakwa.

Spring Rain nodded again. "What do you think?" she asked suddenly, smiling at the little girl.

"I think," Sakwa said seriously, "that you should have who you want to have."

They were halfway down the path when Sakwa suddenly pointed across the desert. "Who is that?" she asked.

Spring Rain looked up, startled. Off in the distance she saw a tiny figure, and drifting toward them like blowing dust was a thin strain of flute notes. "That is . . ." she said, "it must be!" She turned with the baby, tugged on Sakwa's arm, and started running back to the village.

"Who, who, who?" Sakwa called out with every step.

"Don't you remember?" Spring Rain asked. "He is the peddler! We give him our pots and skins, and he gives us things that have come from far away."

"He has those little dolls?" she asked excitedly.

"He might. Do you have anything you could give to him?"

174

Sakwa thought carefully. "I made that small pot that is pretty. Do you think he would take that?"

"He probably wouldn't give you very much for it, but it might be worth a doll. You'll have to ask," said Spring Rain.

In the plaza, Spring Rain shouted, "The peddler is coming! The peddler is coming!" and Sakwa joined in, her small voice shrill with excitement.

All the people came out from where they were working. Some men came up from the kiva; the people in the fields were already coming up the path. Even Anasan came out on his ledge to see what was happening. "Sakwa," said Spring Rain. "You watch the little ones and make sure they don't crawl off the edge. I have to go tell Anasan." The little girl nodded, feeling important with her responsibility, and Spring Rain ran up the ladders.

She was breathless when she reached the ledge. Anasan smiled at her. "What is the excitement?"

"We saw the peddler, playing his flute."

"That is good," said Anasan. "Yala Tawe has not come in a long time. He went by our village last summer. It has been two summers since he's been here, and we need his supplies."

Anasan still had the sharpest eyes in the village, and he could spot the peddler now. "Yes," he nodded, "it is the same one. He has traveled this same road many many summers, as many as he has lived. He does not need eyes to find the path. He knows many people and many stories. I hold the wisdom of our village, but he brings us wisdom of the far lands."

Spring Rain looked down and saw that Sakwa was ignoring the little ones. She stood up. "Anasan, I have to get back to the children."

"Go, then," he said.

She scrambled down the ladders, hardly noticing the holds.

Sakwa was looking over all the pots she had made, trying to decide which she would try to trade. Spring Rain picked up the baby and Tsira, and told Sakwa to come with her up on the roof. They went up, pots and all, and watched the peddler climb up the path to the village. It was exciting to see the formal welcoming. But it was not proper for the children to be around when he was being offered food and drink. So they sat back and waited.

When the peddler had eaten and rested, he opened his many bags and spread out his wares. He had pots and baskets that he laid on splendid blankets. He had seeds and beads and many carved tokens. Around his neck hung an ornate necklace of turquoise and painted wood. Red, green, and yellow feathers hung from holes in his ears. Everything about him was strange and exotic.

Sakwa clutched her best pot and waited while one by one the villagers traded their own work for special goods. When it was finally Sakwa's turn, Spring Rain gave her a little push. Sakwa started forward saying, "Do you have a doll?"

Yala Tawe ran his empty eyes up and down the little girl. She looked terrified. "And what do you have for me?" he asked.

Hands shaking, Sakwa thrust her small pot toward the old man. His hands were open, but not quite ready. The pot slipped between his fingers and fell, shattering on the hard ground. Sakwa shrieked, and ran away, crying. Spring Rain longed to go and comfort her, but here were the pieces of a broken pot to clean up, and an old man who couldn't see.

"She had a pot she was trading for a doll," Spring Rain explained, "but you dropped it. She has gone now."

"I did not touch it," said the peddler. "It was not I who broke the pot."

Spring Rain looked into his pitiful face. This is the man whom the whole village respects, even more than Anasan. But this man thinks more of himself than of a small child. She was disgusted. "About that doll," she said, and she carefully handed him her best basket. She had planned on getting seeds, and maybe an extra turquoise stone for her bracelet. But now she bargained hard and got the peddler to relinquish his finest doll. It even had clothing and a painted face. She made the exchange and gave no thanks.

When she finally found Sakwa, tucked between a wall and the corner of a house, the little girl was asleep. Her face was splotchy with dirt and tears and red from crying. Tenderly, without waking her, Spring Rain laid the doll in her arms.

CHAPTER XXVII

James and Kyaro stopped early in the afternoon, when the sun was only halfway to the horizon. Kyaro stripped off his pack and set it down near several yucca plants. He hacked off some branches with his stone knife. Then he handed the knife over so James could cut some more. Kyaro found a large rock and pounded out the yucca with a stone until it was just a mass of fiber.

When he had finished, James imitated him.

But the next part, rolling and spinning the fibers between his hands to make a cord, took more practice. James tried for a while and just made a mess. So he gave up and helped Kyaro instead by holding the fibers and letting him spin them.

After a couple of hours of this tedious work, they had about fifteen feet of sturdy rope. Kyaro fashioned a kind of trap out of sticks and rope. It was sprung by a delicately balanced stone upset by a thin cord across the opening. Kyaro laid the rabbit carcass, with most of the meat stripped off, in the trap for bait.

They set up camp far enough away so their movements wouldn't frighten any animal. James was careful to collect a substantial pile of wood and stack it around the fireplace. They sat and played dominoes in the soft sand while they waited.

They didn't notice when the great shadow flew across their backs, but they heard the shrill *squawk* and the thump of the stone.

Both of them were up and running without a word. In the trap lay a huge eagle, its foot tangled in the trigger cord, its head under the red sandstone rock.

Kyaro choked back a scream and ran off. James took one look, and ran after him. At the camp site they looked at each other. It was horrible to see an eagle, which should be free and flying all powerful in the air, trapped dead under a rock. James felt numb.

But it was stupid to leave the bird there. He had a lot of meat on him, and his feathers were beautiful. Kyaro was sitting in a lump. James put his hand on his shoulder. "I'm going to need your help, Kyaro," he said in English, then he said, "You come," in Anasazi so Kyaro would understand. The boy stood up, got his stone knife, and went after James.

James pulled apart the trap and carefully lifted off the stone. The sight was horrible, and he tried not to look at it. He reached out his hand for Kyaro's knife.

"Sorry, old bird," he said, as he hacked off the bloody head and covered it with sand. "Now what?" he asked Kyaro. The boy understood the question, and he showed James the movements, explaining very clearly what to do. But he wouldn't touch the bird.

So James made a small slit in the breast skin, where

the feathers were thin, and peeled it back, cutting gently through the connecting tissue. Another slit and he peeled back some more. James tried not to get any blood on the feathers. This was going to take a long time, but Kyaro wouldn't lift a finger to help. He just squatted there, next to James, coaching him with words and movements.

"Bird-you, you-bird," he explained in very simple Anasazi.

"It's my bird," said James in English. "Okay, suits me."

He spoke to the bird as he cut away the skin. "I don't know what we were trying to trap," he said, "but it sure wasn't you. You look like you've been around a long time. But you're awfully skinny." There was no fat under the skin, and even the muscle looked gaunt. "You must have been pretty hungry to go after a dead rabbit. You sure have lovely wing feathers." He stroked the tips, noticing the lacy brown pattern on each feather. He was glad that the eagle's eyes were buried under the sand.

When the skin was peeled off, James took it and the carcass back to camp. Kyaro brought James to a dry creek bed nearby. At the edges, under the lip of the bank where it was shaded, there was a line of gray clay. Kyaro scooped out as much as he could hold, and James did likewise.

They took the clay and spread it over the bird. When Kyaro's hands were free of the mud, he told James to hold on, and he ran off for a few minutes. He came back with pieces of plants—yarrow and sage and some things James didn't recognize. He stuffed these herbs under the clay, then they sealed up the meat.

All night the clay eagle roasted on embers left from a big fire. In the morning, the clay was as hard as a rock, and the boys were starving. They cracked open the pot and feasted on the stringy, juicy, deliciously flavored bird. Kyaro might have felt remorseful about killing the beautiful eagle, but he was too hungry to waste the meat.

They put their water together in one jug and drained the juices and leftover meat into the other. James put the skin and feathers on top of his pack, all salted and sanded to dry.

The great mesa was way behind them, to the south, when they came to the road. The sandy soil had been cut through to the bedrock about the width of a full city street. It went southwest as straight as an arrow. James was amazed. Their path ended in six steps leading down to the road, and they sat for a minute in the shade of the steps.

They had a mouthful of stew, then started off along the road, heading into the sun. *It took a lot of digging to make this road*, thought James. *It is nice to know that other people are out there.*

The going was so much easier. James's legs felt like flying over this smooth, soft road. The sun was off their skin and out of their eyes now. James was starving and numb with thirst, but, aside from that, he felt as if he could go on forever.

They didn't build a fire that night; they just curled up next to each other for warmth and slept in the shadow of the moon on the hard rock road.

The morning was bright, and James woke up before Kyaro. He covered the boy with his own blanket to keep off the chill, and wandered down the road to find a way up to ground level. With the road a good six feet below the level of the land around, he felt as if he were in a canyon, unable to see. Not too far along, he found a narrow crack that he could squeeze through. He stood at the top, listening to a couple of meadowlarks flirt, and watching the sun break over a butte standing like two people with their heads bent together, talking.

And then, with the force of thunder, it hit him. That butte was the Navajo Twins. He was home. This was the view from his bedroom window. He'd know those rocks anywhere. Seeing them caught him in the pit of his stomach. James stared until his eyes hurt, and slowly realized what was missing. There were no houses. There were no people. It was as if all this while, he'd been here suspended in some sort of glass bubble of his own time. Now that glass shattered. Here he was, looking at his home, at the hills he'd played in since he was a child. But everyone was gone! This land was where he had lived; there should have been houses!

He sat down heavily on the red earth and didn't do anything but stare at those two pinnacles of red stone. From somewhere deep within him a thought burst out, *I'm hundreds and hundreds of years ago. I'm before America, before Columbus or Coronado, even before the Navajos.* The thought made him laugh at himself. He picked up a handful of the red dust and looked at it sifting into the dry cracks of his fingers. He flung the dirt to the ground as if he'd been burned. He was holding death.

And then despair overwhelmed him as he realized he had no idea how to get back. There was no ring, no genii, no time machine to warp him back to the future. What about Grandad? What about his mother? What about his own future?

So if he never went back, what was here for him? Spring Rain and Kyaro liked him, but the villagers barely tolerated his presence. They treated him like he was a thief after their food. This wasn't his home, and he didn't see how it ever could be.

At last he wrapped his arms around his legs and buried his head in his knees and knew what he was feeling. He was afraid. He was just plain scared.

Kyaro found him there. "James," he said quietly, "let's go home."

James understood every word Kyaro had said. Only one didn't make sense now—that word, *home.* He could never go home.

CHAPTER XXVIII

The villagers were discussing James with the peddler. He was a wise man, and he knew the stories of their village. He had come to them almost every summer, for many, many summers, longer than anyone could remember. He knew many villages in this way; he knew many languages. The people he spoke to were friendly people. The only language he could not speak was the tongue of the angry ones from the north. So the villagers trusted him.

As much as Spring Rain resented being the subject of discussion, she could understand why they sought the humpbacked peddler's advice. Everyone in the village deeply respected Anasan, but sometimes they needed the truth confirmed by someone else.

The peddler leaned on his walking stick as they told him how Spring Rain had come down that day with the stranger. Spring Rain was standing in a doorway, listening.

"He was dressed like one of us, but he brought nothing with him."

"His backside was as white as a plucked turkey."

"He spoke a strange tongue."

"He brought the rain."

"That is what Anasan says. When he came into the village, the rain stopped."

"He followed Spring Rain and worked like a woman by her side."

Spring Rain wanted to press her hands against her ears. They swarmed like buzzards over a carcass, trying to tell their own part of the story.

"He has green eyes."

The peddler said, "What was that?" At once the group was silent.

The person who had spoken said again, in his quiet voice, "He has green eyes. You can see right through them. Green as the first sprout of corn."

"They glow, they glow in the dark," someone added.

"How do you know? You've never seen him in the dark. He is always with Anasan."

The chatter became overwhelming, trivial.

Spring Rain realized that if she were going to continually come to the defense of James, she would have to know one thing. Would he leave as suddenly as he came, or would he stay? If indeed the song had brought him, then it would take him away. But if she were to sing the song and nothing changed, just as no rain fell for her asking, then she would know. Beyond that she dared not think.

So she understood what had to happen. They would lie together and make the child, for that was more important than any thoughts or feelings she may have.

Then she would take him back to the top of the mesa. She would sing the song again, and if he went away, that would be the end. But if he stayed, they could burn his things, and she would bring him down. She would stand up to the whole village and take him as her man for as long as they both should live.

She left the hut. No one saw her. They were too involved in their discussion to notice anything. She climbed up to speak to Anasan, to share the weight of her decision.

When she was finished talking, Anasan was silent for a great while. When he spoke, it was low and quiet, but she could feel the excitement and determination in his voice. "My mooyi," he said, "you know and I know that it was the song that brought the man James. With him came the rain. He is strange, not of our people. But the song called him, so he belongs to the song. He is a man of your singing. Your seed must grow a man who is able to understand far more than an ordinary man. He will need to be able to speak and join with new peoples when the village makes its last journey. He will need the courage to cross the unknown, to cut fields from untilled soil."

Anasan paused. Spring Rain's skin tingled at his words. This, then, was the beginning. Anasan had never spoken with such detail before; he just alluded to something great, without using clear words.

"So this is what I say to you, young Rain of the New Season." His voice was firm and round. "This is the man you were meant to have. It does not matter if he can run or shoot or climb or fly. He can travel great distances without fear, and speak to people who are as strange to him as he is to them. All things have a pattern, and this is woven as if in cloth."

"But will he stay?" asked Spring Rain.

"That," said Anasan, "is for the villagers and the song to decide."

"Look!" said Spring Rain. The humpbacked peddler had climbed up on a rooftop and was preparing to make a speech. She touched her grandfather on the shoulder and ran down the ladders so she could hear.

"As for the stranger James," the peddler said in a commanding voice, "he has gone out with his challenger to slay an animal. They believe the size and quality of the pelt will determine the winner."

The villagers nodded.

"But I believe there is more to a home than bringing in pelts."

This brought laughter.

"There is also how the pelts are spent. Let the real winner be decided by what he chooses from my array of wares to fill his new home. I will go down and be the first to greet them at the path to the cliff."

There was loud agreement. Spring Rain was horrified. Now Kyaro's plan might not work. There was no possible way she could get around the peddler to warn James and Kyaro. She went slowly back up to Anasan to tell him the news.

CHAPTER XXIX

It was faster going back, because they had the road for almost all the way. Late that afternoon, they turned off the road and cut across the desert again. They ate a light dinner and slept by their fire, and by the middle of the next day they had their own mesa in sight.

James thought about Spring Rain while they were running toward "home." He had never felt so much a part of a girl. She was pretty, but it was more than that. She was lodged inside him like a thorn in the sole of his foot. Except she stuck right between his ribs, making him laugh, making him weep, he was so tender.

Kyaro had gotten ahead of him. Once James could find his own way, he slowed to a walk and let Kyaro keep running. When he reached the base of the path up the cliff to the village, Kyaro was standing there talking with a crooked old man. The man's belongings were spread out on the path, as if for display. Kyaro had his bag down and was showing the man his rabbit skin. James stopped so he could see what was going on without getting involved.

Kyaro asked a question, and the man opened a pouch and took out some seeds. Kyaro felt them and bit them and smelled them, and asked a lot of questions. Finally he was satisfied with his selection. He handed the man his rabbit skin. The peddler felt it carefully and nodded.

Then their conversation turned. The man jerked his head toward James, asking a question. Kyaro called him over and introduced him. "James," said Kyaro.

"Jams," said the man, nodding. "Jams."

Kyaro didn't correct him.

The old man said something, and when James didn't respond, he beckoned with his hand and said, "Jams." So James stepped forward and stood before the old man with his pack on the ground beside him.

The two men, one young, one old, stood in front of each other without talking. James saw wrinkles. Skin that had stretched over cheekbones sagged like empty pockets. Tough ash brown skin that must have once been tight as a drum over the bony chest was now as loose as an old woman's dry breasts. But if all his body was dripping with age, his eyes were not. With searing, cold perception, the clouded gray eyes stared into James's own, understanding secrets James didn't know he had.

Then, as the old man reached out, groping for James's hand, it struck him that those dull eyes that saw everything saw nothing. This old man was blind.

James held out a hand and let his fingers answer the questions that his words could not.

Then the peddler spoke. Phrase after phrase, his words poked James, prodded him, shouted then whispered in all kinds of tongues. James had no idea what he was supposed to do. Even Kyaro didn't understand a word; he stood there openmouthed.

Finally, the old man made a statement in Kyaro's own language. After that barrage of unfamiliar words, the melody sounded clear to James, though the meaning was not. Kyaro recoiled from the words as if hit by a stone. He looked from James to the old man and back to James. His face clenched with tears, and he burst out saying, "No, no, no!"

Slowly, calmly, the old man offered his explanation. James heard what must be the sounds of his own judgment. It became clear to him what was going on. He was a foreigner. He did not speak a language of any of the friendly peoples; therefore, he must be a stranger. And strangers are dangerous.

James heard it all, then he heard Kyaro agree. James was shocked. He looked at the boy.

Kyaro was voicing agreement, but just as he teased Spring Rain, he mocked this man. He smiled warmly at James. This humpbacked peddler must be someone important, but Kyaro was standing up for his friend.

When the old man was finished denouncing James, he stood there leaning on his stick and sucking his gums. James pulled his eagle skin out of his pack. English could do him no harm now that his lot was cast. "Hey, old man," he said, "how much will you give me for this?"

The gnarled fingers felt the skin. They touched each long feather, feeling the shape and the length. Then he stood up as straight as his crooked back would allow, and held the skin out to Kyaro. He barked a sharp question.

Kyaro answered quietly, and he flashed a frightened look at James. The man asked another question, and Kyaro told him the story, remaking the trap with his hands in the air, and setting the stone. He told how James had removed the bird and skinned it, and how they had cooked it.

Here the man interrupted. So Kyaro brought him the jug with the last of the juice and the meat in it. The old man squatted down and proceeded to eat and finish all of their food. James was furious, but Kyaro fed him with questions. The old man grunted in response, his toothless mouth full of the meat.

James started going over the old man's goods with his eyes, seeing what there was to interest him. Woven blankets, small clay pots, some fancy loin cloths, bright feathers, and, escaping from a leather pouch, a string of turquoise beads. He reached for the beads.

"Aiyu!" The old man's voice caught his hand. He had pretty sharp ears. James reached out again and took the bag with the beads. It was elegant. Two beads of turquoise, then a small white shell. He could just picture Spring Rain with it dancing around her neck as she walked.

"This would be a fair trade," he said. "That eagle skin has lots of beautiful feathers."

The man held one bead up, then pointed to one feather. So, one for one. Okay. James counted the feathers while the man counted the beads. Then they switched.

Counting only the large primary feathers, the eagle had five more feathers than the necklace had beads. James smiled. He looked over at Kyaro to see if he approved. His face looked hurt, as if James had betrayed him. What was up? Wasn't he supposed to sell the skin? Or shouldn't he buy a necklace like this? He wondered if Kyaro knew the necklace was for Spring Rain and was jealous.

Then he remembered what Kyaro had purchased with his skin. Seeds, food for the village. So here James goes, spending his whole valuable skin on something that is purely decoration. No wonder Kyaro was upset. Thinking of all this, James fingered the beads. He still felt he needed them; he needed to give them to Spring Rain.

Well, he still had five feathers left. James reached for the pouch with the seeds and set it in the old man's hands. The old man opened the seed pouch and poured a pile of seeds into James's hand.

James turned to Kyaro. "You take," he said in Kyaro's tongue, and he gave the seeds to the boy.

A warm grin spread across Kyaro's face. He thanked James.

The old man interrupted, asking Kyaro a question. "Yes," Kyaro answered, "James gave the seeds to me."

When they finally reached the village, it was dusk, and smoke drifted lazily out of the kiva holes. There were a couple of fires on the terrace where the women gathered.

"Spring Rain," called James. She smiled at him, but she was busy. The disappointment hurt. He'd been gone so long, he at least wanted to be welcomed back. Besides, he wanted her support. He was afraid the peddler was going to say that James couldn't understand any language, and then what would the villagers do?

James walked in the shadow at the edge of the square and climbed up to Anasan's house. The old man was sitting inside by his fire pit, oblivious to what was going on in the village. What a nice position to be in, thought James. He went in and sat down on his own pallet, feeling how much more comfortable it was than the hard ground he had been sleeping on for the past four days.

Anasan said something that sounded like, "So, you're back. How was the trip?" or something equally mundane but comfortably welcoming. James looked into his sharp old eyes, and was suddenly glad that he was there. He smiled at Anasan.

"You know, you remind me a lot of Grandad," he said warmly. "You two are not at all alike, but there's something . . ."

Anasan, listening to James's musings, cracked his papier-mâché face with a smile. James had never seen any expression other than the controlled, thoughtful look. He was surprised and pleased. He imagined himself sitting at the kitchen table with his mug of coffee, telling Grandad about the day. So he spoke to Anasan in the same way. So what if he couldn't understand. James told him all about the trek, where they had gone, about the rabbit and the eagle, and finally he told him about the necklace. He pulled it out of the pouch on his belt and showed it to Anasan. "It's for your granddaughter," he said, "Spring Rain."

Anasan turned his face up from the necklace to look at James. He smiled briefly, but it was warm and encouraging. He was glad this treasure was going to his only granddaughter. But then his face became as stern as a stone, and he put the beads back into James's hand. *This gift was not wise.*

I know. James smiled and nodded. *I also bought some seeds, but I gave them to Kyaro.* He remembered the word for corn, and tried to explain, but it wasn't very clear.

James heard it first, the strains of eerie, echoing music as it floated up and in and out of the cracks of the cliff to Anasan's hut. But when the tones grew stronger, it was like the Pied Piper's seductive melody. Anasan leaned forward, straining to hear, then stood up, reaching for James's arm. *He must be tired,* James thought. *He has never asked me for help before.* Leaning on the boy's shoulder, Anasan shuffled out of his hut and onto the ledge.

He walked with James clear to the end. Then he let go of James's arm and gave him a push, as if to say, "You first."

"No way, Anasan," James balked. "I don't want to go down there. And you are crazy if you think you're going to climb down!"

But, crazy or not, that was Anasan's idea. The wailing flute music floated up and absorbed them, so the climb down was almost a dance.

James took a step and then held his arms up to form a cage for Anasan to step into. And down they went, step by step, with James holding his breath lest the ancient man slip. His old bones shook with the strain, but each step was secure. After the rock wall, the ladders were simple.

But though the peddler's music was alluring to Anasan, James was wary. Anasan pushed ahead, and descended the final ladder alone. James stayed where he was, in the shadows on the rooftop, and watched Anasan's entrance.

There was an audible breath as all the villagers who had come out to hear the peddler play his flute saw Anasan arrive. He passed through the crowd and approached the crooked peddler. The flute hung from his hand like a stick. But when Anasan said something to him, he brought it to his lips and blew, softly at first, and then a jaunty off-center melody. A few men started a line dance. Soon others joined in, and James could pick out both Kyaro and Spring Rain, laughing and singing with the whole village, dancing rings around the older men. Finally, even Anasan broke away from his austere position next to the flute player and joined the dance, his slow, shifting movements just an echo of the steady rhythm of the adults and the wild movements of the children.

When the dance ended, all the people settled on the ground like dust. They were leaning comfortably against a wall or down on one elbow. The children curled up against their mothers, and even Anasan sat down with a back as straight as a stick, with Spring Rain's head against his shoulder.

In a sing-song, the crooked peddler started to tell a

story. His voice ranged high and low, and his hands made sweeping gestures. He said something; there was a reaction among the people; then Kyaro stood up, smiling and twisting on his heel. The peddler stepped back and let Kyaro tell his part. And this story James understood, since he was in it. There Kyaro caught the rabbit, skinned it and ate it. There they fought off a ring of wild coyotes. There they built the trap and set it.

Then Kyaro hesitated. But he had to say it: An eagle flew down and got caught in the trap. James took it. James severed its head. James skinned it and brought it back to camp. Then Kyaro grinned as he described how they caked the bird with clay.

James pulled out the beads and looked at them in the dim light. They were lovely. Not highly polished, not perfectly round, but the blue-green color was as deep as the sky and shot through with white. Each shell was different, some lined with black, some lined with lavender pink or purple. It was beautiful. He hoped Spring Rain would like it.

He looked up at her, sitting with Anasan. The old man touched Spring Rain on the shoulder and pointed to where James was standing. Very quietly, she slipped through the people and was beside him. "Let's go up," she said.

CHAPTER XXX

The two of them climbed up to Anasan's ledge. After Kyaro finished his story, Yala Tawe would tell the village what James and Kyaro had bought and show what they had traded. Spring Rain didn't want to be in the middle of things when the village decided her future for her. From up here, she could still hear the important things that were being said, but she didn't get the whispers and the gossip.

"Spring Rain." James was touching her arm.

"Don't talk now," she said. "Wait until they are finished."

James was silent, but he brought his arm around her and held her to him. They were in darkness back here in the cave; even if someone looked up here, they wouldn't be seen. She leaned into his arm, relaxed and excited at the same time.

Here it was. Kyaro was finished, and the peddler stood up. "I met the two young men on their way into the village," he said in a slow, storytelling voice. "Kyaro showed me his rabbit pelt. It had a thick, deep fur. He

197

chose for it a selection of my finest seeds, which are guaranteed to grow with the minimum of water." The village shouted their approval.

"Spring Rain." James tried to get her attention again.

She looked, and he was holding a pouch out to her. She took it from him and held it on her lap, then turned back to listen.

"And the stranger, Jams, who speaks none of the languages of the friendly people, brought me this." With a dramatic flourish he drew out the eagle skin. Spring Rain looked at James with pride.

"For this flock of feathers, he chose no food, no cooking pot, but a string of turquoise. A decoration. With the few feathers he had left, he took a handful of seeds as well and gave them away to his rival, Kyaro."

"I think the decision is clear. A man cannot feed his family on pretty stones."

There was loud clamor, and one voice came clear. It was a woman: "A man cannot keep a wife on food alone!" The people laughed.

Spring Rain looked down at the pouch in her lap and looked at James. She hardly dared to open it. But she untied the strings and pulled out the beads of turquoise. It was splendid. She had never seen anything so beautiful. James helped to tie it around her neck. She fingered it. The shell in the center was slightly larger, and it fit right into the cave of her throat.

Then she turned her face to him and touched his lips with hers. The turquoise stones rustled on her neck as she moved. "Let's go up to my room in the rock," she said, standing up.

James followed her up Anasan's ladder. He had never been up to the room in the dark before, but she led him slowly.

They sat in the chamber, just holding each other for a while. He was funny; his fingers were cold, but his chest was pumping hot. Spring Rain took his hand and rubbed each finger, making them soft, making them warm.

James held his fingers out straight, and matched her hand with his. His hand was so much bigger; her fingers fit into the center of his hand like a child's. He took her hand and held it against the wall and traced around it with a sharp stone. There was enough moonlight to show the white tracing on the red rock wall.

Spring Rain took her hand down and turned to James. She was ready. She could see from looking at him that he was as well. She unwrapped her hair from the whorls around her ears and shook it so it fell all the way down her back. James said something lovely in his own tongue and touched her hair. She brought it over her shoulders and it covered her like a dress. James smiled into her eyes and pushed her hair back over her shoulders. Then, as gently as if he were painting a delicate pattern, he touched her breasts. They had never felt so tender.

As he took her in his arms and laid her down on the rock, she was overwhelmed by a flood of relief and joy. She felt laughter and tears burst out of her as he touched her skin. She felt a child being made, and she embraced him.

CHAPTER XXXI

James opened his eyes. He must have drifted off to sleep. Spring Rain's head was resting on his shoulder, her arm was around his chest, and her leg was pulled up on his. She was asleep.

He brought his arm around and stroked her hair away from her face. It must be late, but the sounds of music and dancing still drifted up from the village. Eventually the flute stopped playing, and the singing dwindled to a few men. Spring Rain was awake now, but she hadn't moved. "Hey," he said quietly, "let's see what's going on down there. I should go help Anasan climb back up." Then he said in her language, "Anasan-home," and pointed to himself. He smiled, still feeling her warmth, and kissed her, and they looked down at the village.

A bawdy piece of song broke out as several men climbed up from a kiva. Anasan and the peddler came out next. They were walking and swaying with their hands on each others' shoulders. Anasan went up first, and they both climbed to the first roof.

James said, "Spring Rain, I need to go help him."

But she put a restraining hand on his shoulder and said, "Wait." At the bottom of the next ladder the two men stood and talked for a minute. Then the peddler turned and spread out his blanket. He must be sleeping there. He called out good night, and Anasan climbed to the second roof and up the ladder that rested against the wall.

Anasan must have thought of something to say; he turned around all of a sudden and called out to the peddler. But the movement jarred the ladder and it tipped away from the wall. In one sweeping arc it balanced straight up for an instant then crashed and shattered on the second roof.

James didn't hear Spring Rain scream. He just heard his own as he saw Grandad fall.

CHAPTER XXXII

She was shaking. James's arms were around her like a band, but he couldn't stop the shaking. Everywhere she looked, she saw her grandfather falling. She squeezed her eyes closed, but still he arched across her vision. "Ai Ai Ai," she screamed in pain, and pounded James and pounded her fists on the rock. When she finished, he held her and rocked her like a baby.

The words came up from below. It was the hump-backed peddler. When she realized what he was saying, all the shaking stopped and she sat up stiffly, listening. He looked like a flame from all the torches the people had brought.

"This is what comes from welcoming a stranger," he said. "You have taken in an unknown, perhaps a witch, and you have lost your seer. Oh, Yai!" he wailed, with a dramatic sweep of his arms. "He was a great one, and now he lies broken and useless as a shattered pot. Anasan!"

His voice was drowned out by the voice of the village, mourning and angry.

"Anasan liked you," Spring Rain whispered to James. "He said you were the one. How could Yala Tawe say things like that about you?" Tears were streaming out of her eyes, and James kissed them away. "You don't understand what I'm saying, do you?" she asked. "But you know this. You must go," she said, slowly, and James nodded.

"We go," he said.

"Yes, we can go," Spring Rain answered. "I'll take you."

She led the way out the other side of the chamber, and slowly, carefully up the cliff wall to the ledge at the top of the mesa. There were his things, sitting still as rocks, covered with red dust. James picked them up.

Silently they climbed over the edge and walked with their arms holding each other, to the place where she stood to sing. They sat down in the soft sand, and James pulled out his strange blanket. He wrapped it around them. It was warm and slippery. They looked at the stars and talked to each other in their own languages.

"How could he just break like that?" Spring Rain said over and over, tears crying. "He is my grandfather, the only one left for me."

James said, "Sing, Spring Rain." So drawing in a breath, she started the corn song that James knew. They sang it together. When it was finished, James lay down in her lap and closed his eyes.

Spring Rain kept singing, every song she knew. The sky was black, but it turned blue at the edges, and she knew that soon she had to sing the one song. *Not until the sky is the color of a cactus flower,* she said. And thinking that, she had to see James's cactus green eyes once more. She bent down and kissed him, pulling his head up toward hers. He opened his eyes, and the stars were in them, and he smiled at her and said her name.

Spring Rain swayed with grief and joy and exhaustion. The sky was pink, bright and opening up. The stars were closing their light for the sun. She stood up and sang. She sang for all the songs she had sung with Anasan. She sang for all she felt for James. She sang to fill the black hole of emptiness without Anasan, and she sang for the beginning of a child. And as she was singing, the song that had been forbidden to enter her mind all this time came coursing out her lips, and the sun burst over the earth. She reached her lonely arms out to the gods. He was gone. They were both gone forever. She screamed.

CHAPTER XXXIII

James was cold. Still asleep, he pulled the sleeping bag around him tighter. But the sun squeezed through his eyelids, and he felt the raw ground under his bare skin and woke up. He pulled the sleeping bag up over his shoulders and stood up, looking for Spring Rain. She wasn't on the top of the mesa. Where did she go?

He didn't have any clothes on; he smiled, remembering last night, and wondered if he had even put the loin cloth back on at all. Then he remembered about Anasan. My God, no wonder Spring Rain was gone. He left his things where they were and went over to the small cave. His loin cloth would be in the rock room.

He was chilly, but he climbed fast. About halfway down he almost fell, because a ridge he thought was there had moved.

Spring Rain wasn't in the room, and it was full of junk, dirt and stones all piled up. But there was her handprint on the wall. She had chipped out all around the edges. When did she have time to do that? James traced around the lines, feeling her small, strong fingers. He couldn't think.

He had to go to the opening and see what had happened, but his stomach clenched. He closed his eyes.

He stepped to the edge and almost fell. His eyes sprung open, and all he saw was a sheer drop down to nothing. Anasan's house was roofless and crumbled. Way down below, there was just a lot of rubble. No houses, no ladders. No people, no dogs, no fires. No Anasan, alive or dead. No Kyaro. No Spring Rain.

He wrenched himself away from the edge and sat under the shelter of the rock, almost hoping the rock itself would slip and crush him.

He put his hand on Spring Rain's rock print; his eyes were so full he couldn't even tell if his hand was shaking. Through the haze, he noticed the handprint of a baby next to Spring Rain's. *Who is this?* he wondered. *Is this for me?* He felt like dust.

After a long time, he went back out the other side. It had started to rain, a slow, gentle rain. James turned his wet face up to the sky and cried.

Naked and alone he climbed down the mesa. The rain made pools of mud out of the dry earth. Numb and unthinking, he somehow put the mesa to his back and ran blindly in the right direction. His mind was full of Spring Rain's song, and his heart was full of her life. He'd given her a child. His feet slapped the mud. Her grandfather had died. Anasan. Kyaro. He'd never been closer to people in his life. Where were they? Where was he?

CHAPTER XXXIV

James stumbled across the desert, oblivious of the rain cooling his toughened skin. He didn't think to eat. He just kept walking and running in the same direction. When it was night, he fell down in an exhausted heap and slept without dreaming. He woke with the sun and kept on going.

If Grandad hadn't been parked by his truck, waiting for him, James probably would have run past, not remembering the point of this journey. But Grandad held him and laid him gently on the back seat of the car and covered him with a blanket.

As if a nightmare had left its dirty fingerprints on his mind, James vaguely remembered a hospital, and tubes with fluids going into his arms. But the arms didn't really belong to him. He wasn't really there.

Sometimes, when Grandad came into his room at home to spoon-feed him, James would think he was seeing Anasan. Then he saw the old man fall and crumble into death, and James would weep. Sometimes he would hear a voice singing so sweetly that he knew

Spring Rain was in the room. He'd call out for her, but Grandad always came.

Once, though, it was his mother. He had this long conversation with his mother, although afterward, he couldn't remember if it had been a dream.

"Are you my mother?" he asked her. He wasn't sure of anything anymore.

"James, why do you do this to me?" she asked. She seemed sad; maybe she was crying. He wasn't sure. "You always seem to be accusing me, as if it was my fault your father went away. Even when you were a baby, and you were screaming, I thought you were saying what a horrible mother I was.

"One day you had a temper tantrum. I think you were three. I was going to take you with me to my show. We were performing at the fair, and I thought you'd love it. But you were playing with your blocks and didn't want to stop. Your grandad said go ahead and leave you, so I did. But I felt terrible, so I came back. You were playing happily. I stood there crying and you didn't even notice me."

"Mom, I was only three."

"I know."

He remembered that her face had black streaks from her mascara running. "So that's why you never came back?" he asked.

She nodded. "I'm sorry, baby. Don't run away again."

"Run away?"

"Shush, baby. I love you."

He thought she sang to him, a lullaby maybe. But he fell asleep again. He didn't really remember.

CHAPTER XXXV

One night he dreamed about Spring Rain. He dreamed that they were down at a river, a big river, rushing fast at their feet. They undressed and went in the water. He pulled her back to him and dipped her head in the water. Her hair came loose, and he poured sweet-smelling shampoo, apricot shampoo, all over her hair. He scrubbed and it lathered, and he rinsed it away. Then they lay in the sun, and her hair was silky and light like a hundred feathers as it blew across him.

When he woke up, he was in his room at home. Home. Where he was born; where Grandad was. The sun came in through the window, and the birds gave their dawn chorus. It was early. He sat up in bed. He felt dizzy and light, as if he'd been sick a long time and his muscles were like a baby's. That word made him think, and he shivered at the thought. His baby.

But he was home.

God, was it all an elaborate dream?

He stood up and went into the bathroom and closed the door. There was a full-length mirror. He looked at himself. He looked so different from them; it was more than the eyes. He was longer and lighter. He looked at his back, and at his bottom, noticing the deep, even color.

The sight was like a shot of menthol to his brain. No tan line! He wrapped his arms around himself and sat down on the toilet, shaking. Then he brushed his teeth and thought about Spring Rain's teeth. They were so awful, but he hadn't even noticed them by the end. His must have been just as bad.

He heard Grandad get up and go into his room.

"James?"

He stood up and opened the door and looked at his grandfather for the first time. "I have something to tell you," he said.

"I'll bet you do!" Grandad came up to James and wrapped his arms around him, welcoming him home.

EPILOGUE

The time has come!" The man was still very young, but he could call together the village with his voice. "I have sung the songs, and the stars have spun their answer. We must leave in the morning."

There was loud objection from the people. Even his mother questioned him. "Don't you think this is a little fast for us? We have to gather our things."

He smiled at her, his mouth serious, but his eyes teasing. "The longer we stay," he said, "the more we quarrel." And to the village he said, "Leave all but the most important items. Pack all the food you can find in light carrying baskets and pack the seeds in small feathers and down. When we stop, we will have fertile land and fast water.

"We will leave with the sun."